I0740363

Mrs. Snoad

Echoes of Life

Including the 2d Edition of Clare Peyce's Diary and As Life Itself

Mrs. Snoad

Echoes of Life

Including the 2d Edition of Clare Peyce's Diary and As Life Itself

ISBN/EAN: 9783337019167

Printed in Europe, USA, Canada, Australia, Japan

Cover: Foto ©Raphael Reischuk / pixelio.de

More available books at **www.hansebooks.com**

BY

MRS. FRANK SNOAD.

*INCLUDING SECOND EDITION (REVISED) OF
"CLARE PEYCE'S DIARY," AND "AS LIFE ITSELF."*

" Ars longa, vita brevis."

$$\mathfrak{Dedicated,}$$

ENTIRELY WITHOUT PERMISSION, TO

MY DOCTORS,

AS AN AMENDS FOR MANY A " MAUVAIS QUART D'HEURE "

THEY HAVE ENDURED AT MY HANDS.

THE LATE H. G. NOYES, M.D.

SIR WILLIAM GULL, BART., F.R.S., &c.

THOMAS MOORE, F.R.C.S.

ERNEST CLARKE, M.B.

DEDICATION.

Who shall be first, where each has done his best?
He who first fought, ere his own shaft had sped.
Strew the immortelles where he lies at rest.
You will not grudge it? Honour to the dead!

Could grateful memories call him back again,
Could human sorrow bid the dead arise,
My tears should fall like showers of quickening rain
From the soft sadness of blue April skies.

Then next—give precedence to rank and age!—
The cool, keen eyes that every question meet,
The softest voice that utters counsel sage,
The softest hand that feels a pulse's beat.

And next?—In truth (and let him carp who will),
Although as yet but half the victory's won—
For patient kindness, quiet thought and skill,
My life at stake! I count him next to none!

And last, for, latest in this weary fight,
No lingering meed my gratitude defers,
Queen of the tournament I dub him knight,
A poison'd needle won his gilded spurs.

PREFACE.

THE weary hours of a long illness, brought on by over-work, have been the parents of most of the following pages. To those who may perhaps think some of the poems are not quite in accordance with the work which laid me prostrate, I can only plead that human nature is many-sided, and there is little chance in such an illness as mine for anything sterner than love and idleness. But for the devoted love and sympathy of husband and friends, and the care and kindness of my doctors, even so slight an effort would have been impossible ; as it is, the proofs have been but indifferently corrected. Still, it has been a pleasure to me to put the book together—it will, I think, be a pleasure to some to possess it ; if it is a pleasure to the reviewers to cut it up—so be it. Not but what I prefer those critics who cut up other people.

"THE FIRS," OLD CHARLTON.

1884.

CONTENTS.

THROUGH THE FURNACE.

CONTENTS.

ΖΩΝΗ ΜΑΡΓΑΡΙΤΩΝ.

A HANDFUL OF VERSES.

Part II.

CLARE PEYCE'S DIARY.

AS LIFE ITSELF.

Part I.

ECHOES OF LIFE.

ECHOES OF LIFE.

PROLOGUE.

WHAT would I give for health?   Ay, all I have!

Each dear delight that gave existence zest,—

Bury the present in a dreamless grave,

Nor shrink from months, nay, years, of weary rest—

Forsake the charm of Friendship's sweet behest,

Lay hope and purpose like worn garments by,

Nor heed the calls of pleasure and of ease,

Nor crave fresh air and sunshine,—and to lie

Careless of aught, except the leafy trees

And the broad bosom of the cloudless sky !

Nor listen to the hurrying rush of feet,

The noise and bustle of the world's great Fair—

Nor court the press of work—though work is
    sweet ;
Nor long, and wait, to hear upon the air
The sonorous ring of Life's triumphal march,
And the loud plaudits of the busy throng ;
Nor yearn with heated brow and quick heart-beat
For the hot winds which fan success along,
And break the clouds of Hope's glad rainbow-arch.

   *   *   *   *   *

Ay, I am willing !   Suffer and be strong !
Was said by sweeter counsellor than I !
And what ?   Keep silent !   Leave my gift of song !
Nay that I cannot, cannot till I die.

Fain would I give the promise that you ask,
But 'twould be like the mist before the sun—
A weary trouble—never-ceasing task—
Yet frail as cobweb by the spider spun.
All other gifts are mine to leave, this *one*
Is part of me, my very self and soul—

Till life is over, till Time's sands are run
It is not mine to question or control.
The harp was laid within my heart of hearts,
And every pulse sweeps lightly o'er a string,
No rivulet that in the forest starts
Is fed more surely by a hidden spring ;
Through all Time's troubles—all its toils and
    smarts—
To bear them patiently—I needs must sing.

Whom do I sing for—ay, in truth, a few.
Past is the time of songster's triumph-gains.
The quiet nook, where Poesy once grew,
Like a tall lily fed by shade and dew,
Is iron-laid for nineteenth century trains.
To catch the world's applause one way re-
    mains :
Clear, trenchant writing, like a sword of steel,
Fearless of critics—careless of mere pains,
But cleaving *facts* in twain from head to heel.
Such writing must be prose to make men feel ;

And I have won some laurels in my time.
Why leave it then—for this light bark whose keel
Scarce cuts the waves of famous verse and rhyme ?
Ay, but I cannot tell you !   Ask the thrush
Why he pipes on despite the beating rain ;
Or ask the nightingale on yonder bush
Why she pours forth her song of love and pain—
They only sing—nor answer make again !
It is but few who listen—only they
Whose chance or leisure brings them down the lane.
To those whom chance or leisure brings my way
I sing my song—and trust that the refrain
May find that echo in their pulses beat
Which makes the wild bird's careless song so sweet.

NEW YEAR'S EVE.

HARK ! the joy-bells loudly ring !
And the echoes answer faintly ;
To our hearts the angels sing
    Carols saintly.

" Fresh the year before you lies !
Stainless as a snowdrop's centre;
Ere the world its whiteness dyes,
      Let God enter !

" Evil thoughts, temptation's snares,
Flee His presence pure and holy ;
Build the new year up with prayers,
      Meek and lowly.

" Leave the past its envious strife !
Leave it all its sin and sorrow !
Lead a fairer, better life,
      From to-morrow."

To the angels' silent song
Human voices chant in chorus :
" Lo ! a new year, young and strong,
      Lies before us.

" Fortune on the threshold stands,
Beck'ning us to follow after—
Dealing with impartial hands
      Tears and laughter.

" Too oft, in the cloudy past,
Have her smiles been vainly bidden ;
In this year, may be, at last,
    They are hidden.

" Patient work and honest trust,
Endless energy and striving,
Sometimes gain toil's homely dust,
    Golden hiving.

" Dreams of innocence and youth,
Dreams, too often, self-deceiving,
Sometimes prove a blissful truth
    Past believing."

Thus Hope dawns with dawning days,
Till the spirit and the letter
Both foretell in different ways—
    " Something better."

May that " something " come to all
Who this world's rough storms are braving,
And to each the blessing fall,
    Each is craving.

REMINISCENCES.

Deep in the trunk of that seam'd old fir,
Half worn by the beat of long summer rains,
The life of the past seems to wake and stir,
That true love-knot still remains !

And all the years that have pass'd since then,
They seem as though none of their tribe had been ;
Once more I stand in that leafy glen
A maiden of sweet sixteen.

Once more, with my life still an unreal thing,
I wait—impatient for woman's prime,
And play at love—till its finger'd string
Strikes an echo out of Time.

And still as the fir-trees sough and sway,
And through the branches the squirrels leap,
That summer's breezes around me play,
And over my forehead creep.

Shut in the heart of that deep, dark pool
The very shadows seem still to lie,
And fringe the edge of the waters cool,
As they did in days gone by.

And through the masses of tangled fern,
And caught in the bells of the foxgloves bright,
The shreds of that sunset seem to burn
As the sunset of to-night.

Was it a summer of long ago ?
Have I but dream'd of an after life ?
Ay me ! for in truth I hardly know
The girl from the sober wife.

Those years of wedlock ! my child at play !
Are *they* the phantoms and *this* the truth ?
Or that dim dream of a summer day
A glimpse of heather and youth ?

" Come, darling."   Ah ! all the visions fly !
And youth has vanish'd amongst the firs,
Some day my daughter may, passing by,
Find out the meaning of hers !

May catch the prelude of Life's great psalm,
May learn the first, faltering notes —and then
God send her after the trustful calm
Which follows the heart's Amen !

ONWARD.

IN olden time the intellects profound
Imprison'd him who said the world went round ;
Succeeding generations hail'd a sage!
And are there none in these enlighten'd days
Who with quick censure, or faint-hearted praise,
Strike down the hand which strives to turn a page ?

Prophetic souls ! who, born before your time,
Catch the faint echo of the far-off chime,
Which Progress in triumphant anthem rings ;
Who with keen eyes can pierce the veil and see
The glorious future of the pure and free,—
Hear the soft rustle of the angels' wings !

Is there much difference betwixt then and now ?
A martyr's halo for reformer's brow,

Then persecuted, *now* " misunderstood :"
Still grey beards wag, and still the past holds all
Her myriad followers in tightest thrall,
Whilst pioneers flash gleams of light and good.

Work on, true souls, brave hearts, and clear, calm eyes;
Leave to the herd the right to criticize,
Their shallow censure, and their judgments dense.
Time turns his hour-glass; the sands roll on;
Lo! ridicule and censure both are gone;
" Fanatic folly " shines out " common sense."

OLD LETTERS.

SHREDS of a brief, bright summer, long flown,
With its burning sunsets, far out of reach,
The trysting-gate by the nuts o'ergrown,
The crimson roses, and copper beech,
And shy, sweet moments too blessed for speech.

The half-form'd plans for the days in store,
Our two lives blended, the twain in one,
And vague, fond dreams, which can come no more
Through winter rime or through summer sun.
Tie up the packet! its work is done.

Like a dew-drop shut in a fading rose,
Youth lies shut in each well-worn fold ;
Yet Time in his flight but more plainly shows
The truth of the story that summer told,
And present joy was the hope of old.

WROTHAM HILL.

THE summer skies wore a leaden frown,
The pitiless rain came splashing down,
As if the deluge had broken out,
As if the clouds were a waterspout ;
Dashing the pebbles from side to side
In puny torrents of sparkling pride,
Drenching us, with a right good will,
As we drove slowly down Wrotham Hill.

" Where can we shelter find ?" said we ;
There was none save an old elm-tree,
Which, stretching forward its branches tall,
Made a dusty track where no rain could fall.
" Pull up, ' Folly !' we'll shelter here,
And laugh at storms till the skies shall clear."
*   *   *   *   *
" You look so pretty, my love !" said he,
" Waiting here 'neath the old elm-tree,

Button'd up in your ulster coat,
With the fleecy woollen around your throat,
Its ample hood drawn over your head,
And your eyes so bright and your cheeks so red."
And then, half dropping the loosen'd rein,
He kiss'd me—softly again, again,
Kiss'd me there in the pelting rain,
With only the squirrels aloft to see,
And the drifting leaves and the old elm-tree,
And the glad birds twittering joyously.

Lovers newly plighted were we,
Waiting there 'neath the old elm-tree?
Nay, my friend — for five changeful years
We'd shared together life's smiles and tears,
Walk'd life's way a united life,
He a husband and I a wife!

HONEYSUCKLE.

THAT grim old oak, whose branches thin and hoary
Were stricken down in ruin long ago,
The summer kisses into fragrant glory
When crooning bees tell many a sweet love story,
And all the wealth of honeysuckles blow.

Round the bare branches, crack'd and gnarl'd and
    seamy,
A myriad trumpets for the elves unfold ;
And far and near there floats a perfume dreamy,
From clustering masses, crimson-flush'd and creamy,
Soft as girls' blushes—deep as molten gold.

Like Hamadryad from the old trunk springing
Forth to fresh youth amid the sweetness there,
Or blue-eyed wood-nymph in wild cadence singing,
My little daughter eager spoil is bringing,
The honeysuckle falling on her hair.

Ah ! when your summer comes to you, my treasure,
And as life's path grows wider to your feet,
Heaven send you gifts in no unstinted measure,
Your two hands full of work's mix'd pain and
    pleasure,
And the soft flushes of love's rapture sweet.

But, more than all, the inner nature waking,
The hidden fragrance yielding to God's sun—
Where other hearts in chill despair are breaking,
And grief and ruin grim, dark wrecks are making
Of lives by gladness into beauty won.

I would not wish for you the narrow prison
The trim-kept borders of the orthodox,
But charity divine from love's own chrism
Fall, red and golden, free from bigot schism,
Like honeysuckle garland on your locks.

CRITICISM.

" VAIN, sounding brass, which a fool has struck,
And deem'd a cauldron the wide world's gong,
No wealthy patron, no stroke of luck,
Could save that clamour and din for long."
So said the critics—and who but they
Could gauge the worth of this new-fledged bard ?
Dip deep in gall, and then write away,
That task is easy, if praise is hard !

" A tinkling jangle of puny bells,
The veriest toy that the world has seen !
A feeble tune that its weakness tells,
Go, slit the skin of the tambourine ! "

So said the critics—and who but they
Should know pure weakness from inborn strength ?
Light up the squibs, and then blaze away,
A bonfire's faggots will yield at length !

Time passes by with his scythe and glass,
And slowly, slowly, he pours its sands ;
Till rising, swelling, the sweet sounds pass
And echo answers from distant lands.
The sounding brass throbs its deep amen,
The tinkling bells sigh their sweet refrain,
Men ask, " The critics ? Where are they then ? "
But Time smiles only—men ask in vain.

SPRING MEMORIES.

COLD old bachelor !   Ay, they're right !
They all say it !—it must be so—
Yet like an arrow cleaving the night,
Like a swallow's swift homeward flight,
Come the dreams of that " long ago."

Once, when the earliest primrose bloom,
Bade the chorus of spring begin,
Love pierced the shadows of wintry gloom,
And o'er the sill of my lonely room,
Let the sunshine come streaming in.

Sunshine strange to my heart and eyes,
Sweet as the April blue which stole
Through the mist of the wild March skies,
Precious as promise of Paradise
To the thirst of a weary soul.

The budding hedgerows of velvet palm
Whisper'd the violets down the lane :
" Look ! see our lover's contented calm ! "
The callow nestlings twitter'd a psalm :
" Hush ! there is Eden on earth again."

But, when the trees donn'd their bridal veil
Rugged Autumn with gifts to crown,
My lady's sighs grew as faint and frail,
My lady's looks grew as wan and pale,
As apple-blossoms which flutter'd down.

And when the roses had sigh'd alas !
Wafting like incense their sweets to God,
They shed their leaves o'er a mound of grass.
Thoughtless footsteps may idly pass.
There my heart lies—under the sod.

A SHOP-HAND.

THE fashion copied in cheaper stuff,
More showy, may be, than neat ;
And a jaunty hat that is gay enough
For the lighted London street.
Young, ay, so young ! and her face still fair,
For a country girl is she.
The smoke still fights with the country air ;
Glad, buoyant hope, with starvation's care ;
The hedgerow bloom, with a rouged despair ;
As yet —'tis purity.

The season's over ! the shutters close
Throughout Belgravia's squares ;
For wearied fashion it seeks repose,
And jaded Life—repairs.

The shops are " slack," so the " hands " must go.
Wages ? Ah ! happy she
Who can find a " house " full enough to throw
The barest crumb of a meal or so,
The scantiest help, now that trade's so slow,
" Half a crown a week, and tea."

Better by far is the merest drudge,
In the meanest service fed,
Than she, who can only toil and trudge,
By fierce temptation led.
But ah ! 'tis too late for turning back,
She is " out of the way, you see,"
She must keep straight on in the chosen track
Whether the houses are " press'd " or " slack ;"
For wholesome service she's lost the knack,
She has tasted—liberty !

Liberty, yes—when—for come it must—
In the awful fight she falls,
Will she seek the skilly and honest crust
In the cheerless workhouse-walls ?

Or will she (for it is easier found,
Where the cruel gaslights burn),
Slip 'mid the wheels as their whirr goes round,
And women's bodies and souls are ground
For bread, such as shocks by the very sound,
Yet meets us at every turn.

Ah! men and women with dainty homes,
As you sip your hock or champagne,
Think of the girl shop-hand who roams
Through the London slush and rain ;
And know that Legion must be their name
Who fall on starvation's brink !
" Their faults ?" may be, but if Christ, who came
To pierce all hearts with His sword of flame,
Had stay'd in Heaven and thought the same,
" Their faults "—Ah ! pause and think.

RHODODENDRONS.

A crimson glow 'mid the dark-green leaves,
A regal harvest of ruby sheaves,
Stretching as far as the eye can see,
Through to the depths of the shrubbery ;

A summer-house, 'neath whose thatch we two
Speak of dreams long past, and of hopes yet new,
Whilst fast without falls the soft spring rain,
And the cuckoo's note cries again, again,

     Cuckoo! Cuckoo!

There is good work done, and good work to do!

Just a last brief talk, just a parting word
With the cuckoo's note in the distance heard;
A swift farewell, then the whizzing train
Back to the whirl of life again!
Yet evermore, 'mid the false, the true,
There rings the echo,

     Cuckoo! Cuckoo!

There is good work done, and good work to do!

CHRISTIANITY.

A GOOD ship sails o'er the waves of Time, with a
    strange and varied crew,
Of every age, and of every clime, of every race and
    hue;

There is every sect which the world can frame, but
    the broad flag floats above,
Which binds in one comprehensive name all the creeds
    which Christians love.

The night is dark in these latter years, and the
    breakers surge and swell,
The storms rage high of men's doubts and fears, and
    the end—ah! who can tell ?
Yet sail on, ship, to the promised land, though thy
    pure white sails are torn,
There is never a rock nor a false quicksand that can
    bring the voyage to scorn.

Sail on ! Though the lightning rends the skies, and
    thy course seems almost o'er,
For the God above hears His servants' cries, and will
    bring thee safe to shore ;
His wrath speaks now in the thunder's might—let
    the erring signals be !
For after the roar and the din of fight, comes a still
    small voice to thee.

And heed not the mist which creeps apace o'er the
    purple fringe of the world,
Where the pirate ships with the future race, all their
    evil flags unfurl'd ;
Take the diamond light of truth for guide, and the
    grand old-fashion'd chart,
And weather the worst that can e'er betide, with a
    brave and hopeful heart.

There is One who watches beside the helm, and the
    storms wait on His will,
Though their cruel anger may overwhelm, He can
    whisper, " Peace ! be still !"
When the right time comes, He His help will send to
    the souls who danger braved,
And they who fight to the bitter end by His faithful
    word are saved.

What matters sect ? so the cause is one, what matters
    race or name ?
Life's battle fought and life's journey done, the
    victory is the same.

Let the details go! let the trifles be! until, free from
    earthly leaven,
The broad flag Christianity is safe in the Courts of
    Heaven.

NEW OWNERS.

BOUGHT the dear old house! Oh! it is so kind,
With workmen busy, to take me over;
There's never a chink in my heart or mind
That some loved stone does not mark or cover.
Cut the lawn away for a carriage-drive!
Well—yes—that cedar has had its day;
But oh! the past seems awake, alive,
With every twig, every leaf and spray.

Throw back the staircase, enlarge the hall,
Ah! new-fledged wealth has most ruthless fingers,
It may be narrow and mean and small,
But in its meanness romance still lingers.
Of course, of course! it is as you say,
You like things modern—I beg your pardon?
No, thanks—not over the house to-day,
But just a peep at the grounds and garden.

This is the dear old lavender-bush !
Nay, don't hurry, just pause a minute ;
Almost I hear the song of the thrush,
And feel my hand with a fond hand in it !
What did you say ?   (How the very sound
Of my own voice startles me !)   Yes, no doubt,
'Twill make a charming new tennis-ground,
When all the rubbish is rooted out.

Here is the summer-house bleak and wide !
Ah, yes, 'tis ugly—a blot, you know —
But how we've loiter'd here, side by side,
Through April rain and December snow.
And—thank you, no—it is late, I think ;
These winter evenings draw in so soon.
I'll just turn back by the river-brink ;
That cannot alter like youth and June.

AFTER ALL.

"Do you remember ?"   She turn'd her head,
Her cheeks flush'd soft with a crimson glow.
" That is twenty years ago," she said.
  " Yes, twenty years ago."

" Many a change has been rung since then,
Many a turn in time's ebb and flow,
Your two lads are both stalwart men
    Since twenty years ago."

" Ay, and *your* girl has her mother's eyes,
Such as her mother's were then, you know ;
And *her* husband counts her his life's best prize
    Like—twenty years ago."

" Your youngest grandchild can run alone,
The elder ones into girlhood grow."
" Ay, but your voice has the same soft tone
    As twenty years ago."

" My face is lined, and my hair is grey,
And youth's hot pulses are still'd and slow ;
Yet, I ask you now, what I ask'd that day,
    Just twenty years ago ! "

" You ask'd me then if I loved you well,
I could not utter the falsehood *No*,
But the bitter truth how dared I tell ?
    'Tis twenty years ago."

" And we both kept loyal to truth and right,
And did our duty." " Ay, that is so !
No shadow lies on our hearts to-night,
      From twenty years ago."

" Yet, though life's downward path we tread,
And evening shadows lengthening grow,
Our love is as fresh and strong," he said,
      " As twenty years ago.

" Our love is fresh, though our heads are grey,
May life's last decade its rapture know ! "
" Yes," she said, " it seems like yesterday,
      That twenty years ago."

PICOTEES AND MIGNONETTE.

PAST are the violets that shyly crept
Behind the tender leaflets of the spring,
Past, the pale primroses which starr'd each cleft
Of budding woods, where new-pair'd thrushes
      sing.

The roses in the sun's embrace have died,
Their luscious beauty, languorous with perfume ;
The stately lilies bow'd their heads of pride,
And sigh'd their souls out in a sheaf of bloom.

Fast comes the waning of the summer's prime,
But on the earth her glory lingers yet,
And scents as sweet as spring or summer-time
Hang round the picotees and mignonette.
The dewy violets which morn has kiss'd,
The throbbing roses, with their cores of gold,
Pass'd with the cuckoo, and are scarcely miss'd,
Though skies grow greyer, riper blooms unfold.

Less fresh and coy, perhaps, but not less sweet,
Less brilliant, not less passionate the hue ;
Youth's early eagerness and quick heart-beat,
Maturity's full rhythm, strong and true ;
They come with all their passion and their pain,
Their mingled web of rapture and regret,
Yet through the autumn mists they live again
In blood-red picotees and mignonette.

FOR EVER.

OVER the glistening sands of Time
A year in its pitiless force has roll'd—
A wave of Eternity, grey and cold,
Dashing out landmarks our hopes had set,
Leaving a broad, trackless desert, wet
With unshed tears which our full hearts hold.

Back to the wearying toil we come,
Like children laden with pail and spade,
To weep at wrecks which the sea has made,
To build awhile, and to struggle on,
Till the hot sun sinks and the day is gone,
And we are panting for rest and shade.

Yet the restless waves never cease their flow ;
Still, still they roll o'er the shifting sand,
And brain's full measure and strength of hand
Lie levell'd out on the placid shore.
The night has come when men work no more,
And we are bound for the shadow-land.

O God ! all these visions of love and joy,
These burning hours of pain and grief,
This ceaseless toiling without relief,
This passionate burden of hopes and fears,
Which make the rhythm of life's long years—
What are they worth in a time so brief ? "

A voice in answer came back to me,
" Live not for time—but Eternity."

A LEGEND.

A DEAD dog lay at fair Judea's gate,
The scavenger of unclean offal he !
And each good Jew, moved with his creed's just
    hate,
Spurn'd the cold carcase right contemptuously.

There were no epithets too foul, too vile,
To heap upon the creature as it lay,
Whose sight could sicken, and whose touch defile,
Such pure disciples of the law as they.

A stranger pass'd and look'd upon the dead,
With Christ's own charity His soft eyes shone,
" Pearls are not whiter than its teeth," He said,
And 'mid the hush of censure, passed on.

Learn thou the lesson!   When all tongues decry
Leave slander, calumny, abuse to them—
It may be that the Saviour passing by,
In His good time, will search and find a gem.

PRIMROSES.

" COUNTRY primroses! fresh and sweet!
Violets! only a penny a bunch!"
A young girl cries, whose weary feet
Tread many a muddy city street,
While rich folk idly dine or lunch.

Repletion theirs! starvation hers!
How long will those pale flowers keep fresh?
If no heart yearning pity stirs,
How long ere she no more demurs
To sink the spirit in the flesh?

Ay! sneer and pass the other side!
But when Christ comes, of this be sure,
'Tis not *her* shame He will deride,
The shame is yours, who have not tried
To keep His blossoms fresh and pure.

MARA.

"I LOVE! I love! for love's the crown of youth!
And she I love is young and fond and fair!
We've vow'd each other constancy and truth,
And all the other vows which lovers swear.
As through the long grass speeds the startled hare,
So through the future's chances flies my life;
Fame, fortune, must be mine, and she shall share
The fruits of all—when she's my own true wife!"

Through the soft silence of the moonlit night
There floated forth a passionate love song,
With trembling notes in very weakness strong,
And throbbing yearnings for the Infinite,

Wild quivering cadence like a soul's unrest,
In breathless longing for that other soul,
And burning passion spurning self-control,
Then fainting, dying in the hopeless quest
Of word or sound by which such love's express'd.

' It is the nightingale !" the lover said,
" I care not for that sorrowful love strain,
The throstle's note is best, who overhead
Pipes her glad welcome to the summer rain,
And trills out hope in every blithe refrain,
For hope and love and youth and joy are one,
Let those court grief who will, I laugh at pain,
Content and peace be mine till life is done."

Ay, but time pass'd, and stole youth in his flight,
Whose tears at parting fell on hair and beard,
To turn the gloss of manhood's prime to white,
And leave the bloom of early beauty scar'd,
And ripen'd manhood's harvesting appear'd
Where passion stood amid the noonday heat,
And with her keen-edged sickle quickly shear'd

The throbbing fulness of the fading wheat,
And turn'd to quivering pain each wild heart beat.

Again the thrush piped her full-throated song ;
The youth who once had listen'd, he was man,
" Ay ! it is blithe ! " he said, " but not for long,
Let youth and hope go blithely while they can !
Far fiercer fires the winds of passion fan,
And loves wakes but within the soul of life ;
The eager brook that down the mountain ran,
Swells to the river's rush of foamy strife."

Through the soft silence of the moonlit night
There floated forth a passionate love song,
With trembling notes in very weakness strong,
And throbbing yearnings for the Infinite,
Wild quivering cadence like a soul's unrest,
In breathless longing for that other soul,
And burning passion spurning self-control,
Then fainting, dying, in the hopeless quest
Of word or sound by which such love's express'd.

" It is the nightingale," the strong man said,
" She sings her song of love as love must be,
And God help those who learn it ; there is spread
For them the thorn of lasting constancy.
Some hearts are ever lock'd, and their soul's key
Is flung in an abyss beyond earth's reach,
May-be perhaps in vast eternity
They'll learn the notes no human voice can teach."

A HAMPER OF FLOWERS.

FAST crowd old memories through summer showers,
Through thrush's melody and glib " cuckoo,"
Of all that has been. Active, stirring hours,
  And work to do.

Amid the rhododendrons' crimson glory
Lie hidden glimpses of a woodland walk :
And pale azaleas tell a golden story
  Of tea and talk.

The foxglove bells rung out by fairy fingers
Chime in soft silence many a bygone tune ;
Within the rose's heart a message lingers
    Of life and June.

The very Marguerites and blossom'd grasses,
Stirr'd by the flutter of the Past's bright wings,
Bring to the Present, careless how time passes,
    Forgotten things.

Then fades the dream.   Alas ! 'tis memory only
Which hides and nestles in each sheaf of bloom.
The waking is so weary ! Sad and lonely
    A dull sick room.

Lonely ?   Ah, no ! with love and friendship cheering.
Sad ?   Nay, not so, when God is over all.
And He who dealt the stroke shows Heaven nearing,
    Whate'er befall.

For as the shrubbery, though robb'd of flowers,
Will burst in blossom for another spring ;
And through the beat of heaviest thunder showers
    The thrushes sing :

So may the Past, like child refresh'd by sleeping,
After a season of lost hopes arise
To find the angels have a watch been keeping
　　　For sunny skies.
And if it be not so—if work and duty
Are over in this world—He knoweth best ;
He gives the flowers grace, and scent, and beauty,
　　　His children—rest.

HEARD AT MIDNIGHT.

OUT on the clear, cold night it rang,
The frosty calm of a still, March night,
Whilst stars above glitter'd keen and bright,
The self-same stars where the angels sang.
Was there no angel to look down then
With a warning word or a pitying touch ?
Or, ay ! God help her ! was it too much
To *hope* for this slave to the lust of men ?

" You've been my ruin !　You'll be my death !"
A woman's voice where the anguish thrill'd,
Whilst I, with pulses half crush'd and still'd,
Could only listen with bated breath.

Yet through the hush and the dead of night
That woman's shriek brought a woman's prayer ;
Pray God it may help her unaware,
And guide her steps to the truth and right.

Ah ! turn away from that piteous wail,
Self-righteous women whose *lives* are clean.
Whose wedded bosoms the icy sheen
Of custom wraps in a coat of mail.
Purse up your lips and draw back your skirts,
In mute avoidance from such as her,
Lest thoughts of pity which move and stir
The frost of your reputation hurts.

Then, welcome him who has wrought the wrong,
If strong of purse or an honour'd name,
Leave *her* the misery, guilt, and shame,
Crush down the weak and uphold the strong :
Give each to each as is fairly due,
She is a woman and he a man ;
Call it pure justice what time you can,
Pray God He may call it justice too.

"THEY SAID."

THE sun sank slowly in the west,
And bathed the beechen boughs with gold,
We thought our lives were fully bless'd,
That night the old, old tale was told.
" 'Tis sweet," they said, " this game of youth,
But love you know, my dears, will fly ! "
And if 'twas false, or if 'twas truth,
I knew not then—not I !

The bees had sought their well-stored hives,
The swallows fled the wintry sun,
But we were happy, for our lives
Henceforth for ever were as one.
They said, " The caged bird seldom sings,
And tired of silence, soon must fly."
And if I'd safely clipp'd his wings,
I knew not then,—not I !

Years went and came. Love tarried still
Through every change of time and tide,
Through weal and woe, through good and ill,
Too true to swerve, too fond to chide.

Those years have taught me all the truth
That real, true love can never fly ;
'Tis sweeter far in age than youth
    Or so say I !

OUR WEDDING DAY.

SPENT is the summer's last, long, golden ray,
Scarce one bright flower remains amid the dearth,
The sky's soft blue is quench'd in cloudy grey,
The wither'd leaves fall on the sodden'd earth.
The year is slowly sinking into rest,
And weeping day succeeds to gloomy night ;
But, ah ! my husband, memories most bless'd
Like guardian angels rain down warmth and light.

Does it remind you of an autumn day
When we stood hand in hand, and side by side,
The future glowing, though the skies were grey,
Our faith and constancy as yet untried ?
Like apple blossoms drifting on the grass,
The scented days of courtship drift ;—but now
We've watch'd the ripening summer onward pass,
And grasp the fruits which cluster on life's bough.

Look in my face as then, and let me see
If you are changed—Love has a subtle sense
When hope fulfill'd fades to satiety,
And passion passes to indifference.
Ay, time brings changes ever in his train,
Our love has changed—to deepen forty-fold ;
The tie that bound us then is now a chain
Of giant strength, yet every link of gold.

The trust that was but fluttering hope at best,
Is now so woven with our inner life
Doubts die ere born, there is no place to rest
Between the hearts of husband and of wife,
Love's rosy feet tread all the thistles down
Which else might spring upon the smoothest way,
And peace and thankfulness with myrtle crown
The bleak November of our wedding day.

Though trials and griefs may in the future wait,
We'll meet them bravely, if we are but spared
Each to the other—for no trial is great,
And no grief crushing when 'tis soothed and shared.

Grief in its way, like joy, but plainly proves
All we have gain'd of tender and of true.
God grant each woman heart that fondly loves,
Its dreams fulfill'd—as mine have been in you.

THE BELLE OF THE SEASON.

" LOVELY ?   May-be !   When the agate's cut
It shows God's handiwork— so does she,
For beauty in every soul is shut,
No matter how sordid the soul is, but
It oft needs cutting before men see.

" Lovely ?   Perhaps ! the camellia's wax
Is nature—though closely akin to art,
The rounded calyx asunder cracks,
The moulded petals their leaves relax,
But 'tis most perfect without a heart.

" Lovely ?   I grant it ! but, oh ! so cold,
No *life* in that marble beauty stirs.
Dogs lick the hand that they served of old !
A slave would shudder when bought and sold !
It matters nought to a soul like hers."

Better the homeliest face which keeps
A world of love in its quiet eyes,
Where like a jewel true kindness sleeps,
And forth from whose smile and glance there leaps
A myriad sparkling sympathies.

Better by far is the gay coquette,
Her dimpling blushes and flirt of fan,
For there's soul behind it—not moved as yet.
But *there*—sure as sun in the heavens set,
A *woman* laughs out at the smile of man.

Better a vixen with well charged lash,
For passion's fury is over soon,
The rageful glare of the lightning's flash,
And furious clang of the thunder crash,
Melt in the warmth of a summer noon.

OUR WEAPON.

WHAT is the mightiest force in the world?
The statesman's scheming of word and brain,
The merchant's treaty of gold and grain,
Sectarian dictates torn in twain,
Or the shell by the thundering cannon hurl'd?

Ay me ! there's a stronger power than each
In the ruling force that rules the world,
A wiser logic than sages teach,
A keener doctrine than bigots preach,
God gave to woman the key of speech,
And the lever force in a sentence curl'd.

Solomon's wisdom fell to nought,
Samson's strength at a word went down,
For Helen a host of heroes fought,
Aspasia, Pericles' laurels wrought ;
And a mother and wife to the rescue brought,
Made Coriolanus spare the town.

And, ah ! for the wisdom of later days !
But peel from actions the outer rind,
And the kernels ripen'd by woman's praise.
The core tastes sweet of a woman's ways,
The true sun shines through a misty haze,
There's always a woman somewhere behind !

Somewhere behind ! but the world rolls round,
And after night comes the red-streak'd dawn.

We can wait—for our feet have touch'd the ground
Where at last the level of truth is found,
And we know by the echo the clear full sound
Of the coming note on the future borne !

Ay, we can wait ! for at last we know
All Nature's noblest works take time ;
Human forces may come and go
With the ocean's ebb and the ocean's flow.
God's measured ways are sure and slow,
But He gives the fruit in the year's full prime !

A SEPTEMBER IDYL.

THE harvest fields will be deserted soon ;
The hour is late—the autumn breeze blows chill,
The hornèd crescent of the harvest moon
    Hangs o'er the hill.

The laden waggons crunch the dusty road,
High to the top with golden grain heap'd up ;
And farm-maids bring, as guerdon for the load,
    A cider-cup.

For what care they if autumn winds are chill ?
Or if, perchance, the evening dews should fall,
The old, old story, is the sweetest still,
    In spite of all.

As sweet when told beneath a well-thatch'd rick,
Whilst owls peep out and eerie bats take wing,
As in the days when leaves and buds are quick,
    And thrushes sing.

A BUGLE CALL.

SWEET seventeen ! Upon the shores of Life,
Its sun-kissed waves just rippling to your feet,
But far off sounds its roar of stormy strife,
Its harshest story murmuring music sweet.
Time stays not, rests not ; soon will turn the tide,
And you a woman—yesterday a child,
For good or ill, with your own hand must guide
Your destiny across those waters wild.

What do you choose ? An aimless, useless life,
For ever cruising in a still Dead Sea,
Wearing your heart out in the ceaseless strife
You needs must wage with dull monotony,

Steering your course by Custom's narrow chart,
Your only compass, What the world will say!
Having no knowledge of life's nobler part,
With every talent wasted—thrown away?

Or do you choose the active and the true,
Rich with the freight of independent thought?
Right gladly done the work God gives to do,
Each separate gift to ripe perfection brought;
An earnest woman, of whom all shall say,
"She won success, and bravely was it won!"
And who, at last, when comes the reckoning day,
Will hear the Master's answer, "Ay! well done!"

ROSEMARY.

On a Picture by Emily Barnard.

As late November rustles through the trees,
And trails her garments on the leaf-strewn walks,
No scent of roses floats upon the breeze,
A few pale blossoms, lifeless, ill at ease,
Hang faded and forgotten on their stalks.

Amid the sighing of the leafless ash
There chirps no song of bird nor croon of bee,
On the grey rocks the restless breakers dash,
For ever mocking with their idle plash
The far-off weird complaining of the sea.

And on the pinions of the northern wind
There come the splashes of the salt sea spray,
That touch my brow, and passing, leave behind
Their baptism of tears, to echo find
In grief, whose passion seems but yesterday.

Chill are the kisses of the waning year!
Chill are the night dews falling from above!
Yet bitter-sweet their memories.   Here we met,
Here where this bush of rosemary grows yet,
Dark as our fortunes, faithful as our love.

'Twas here the hopes which had half lifeless hung,
Dropp'd their stain'd petals, spoil'd by autumn rain,
Their beauty faded when the year was young ;
And wet, grey skies were o'er our future flung :
We parted then—to never meet again.

E.

So with the dews and odour of the sea,

There comes a message of that wither'd past,

This sombre rosemary is one with me,

Its dim, dark memories with my own agree,

Crush'd into sweetness, faithful to the last.

LOYALTY.

HE pass'd the parterre, where the rich tulips
    glow'd
  In colours that shimmer and burn,
Not a thought on the gorgeous exotics bestow'd,
  Or the delicate mosses and fern.
"But here blooms my prize!" he in ecstasy said,
  And a dew-drop roll'd down like a gem,
As he tenderly lifted the pale, drooping head
  Of a little white rose from its stem.

The rest of the flowers shriek'd out in dismay,
  "That choice is the worst you could make,
That rosebud is grieving her whole heart away,
  But the tears are not shed for *your* sake."

" Be mine, then, the task," was his answer, " to bring
  The sunshine those bright drops to dry,
Such tears from a pure, loving heart only spring.
  That heart will be mine by-and-by."

Then they answer'd, "Your rosebud has many a thorn!
  "Ay! Thorns to preserve her for me."
But they laugh'd in derision and pitying scorn,
  " Many more kiss'd that rose before thee!"
Still he answered, " I know not—or knowing, should
      care
  But little who bent o'er my rose,
For to none not right worthy her friendship to share,
  Her petals would ever unclose."

Then they said, " Ay, the rosebud is fair to the eye,
  But a canker-worm gnaws at the heart ;
Pull it off from the stem ; it will wither and die,
  And your vision of beauty depart."
But he said, " On those leaves there was never a stain
  To harbour a canker or blight ;
And pure as the snow, so will ever remain
  Her petals of maidenly white."

Still they urged, " If 'tis pure, 'tis useless and frail ;
    Leave it now where it blossoms to fade ;
We could tell in your ear such a nice little tale,
    To prove what mistakes you have made."
But he answer'd, " Your venomous lies but disgrace
    The lips which no merit can spare,
And deep in my innermost heart I will place
    My white rose—and cherish it there."

Then the rose whisper'd softly, with many a sigh,
    " Suppose what they tell you is true ;
The passionate noon of my first love gone by,
    And only the evening for you ?"
" So be it," he said, " I'd not alter nor change,
    As you are, of my heart you're the queen,
Give me love that like mine cannot waver nor range—
    I envy no one what has been."

The rosebud's soft breath floated forth like a prayer,
    And as her white petals unfold,
The pale, blushing heart in its beauty lies bare,
    With its deep inner centre of gold.

The dew-drops of grief have but freshen'd her leaves,
　　And kept her unscathed from the sun ;
For Loyalty ever full guerdon receives
　　In love which no other has won !

AT THE "GEORGE," WINCHESTER.

WE stood by the quaint, old window-sill,
　　And gazed far down in the bustling street ;
With us, all quiet and calm and still—
　　With them, the throng of hurrying feet.
A hush seem'd over our pulses' beat,
　　He scarce a husband, I scarce a wife.
We whisper'd " Ay, the present is sweet,
　　What of the hurry and rush of life ? "

Amid the toil of our work-a-day
　　Will true love lessen, howe'er intense ;
Romance die out, as the worldlings say,
　　And day-dreams fade into common sense ;
Trust come to shillings and pounds and pence,
　　When fades the moon of this early time,
And we but practise a poor pretence
　　Of youth's first freshness and passion's prime ?

Once more by that window-sill we stand,
And listen to voices and hurrying feet ;
Though years have pass'd, yet still hand in
     hand,
The past seems present, and both are sweet ;
Our lips the words of years gone repeat,
Those words which follow'd our bridal vow,
" Is love illusion and trust deceit ?"
Ah ! there's no need for that question now.

DELUSION.

That love ! the crystal rivulet, which flows,
In drops of cooling, by your life's highway !
That love ! the song which lulls you to repose,
And soothes the evening of a weary day !
Ay, think so ! dream your restful life away,
It is to youth the fates wild visions send,
For youth alone is foolish—so they say,
But love comes once to all, and, ah ! my friend,
He loves the glowing sunlight of noonday.

Some day that rock, struck by divining rod,
Will shrivel at the stroke and fall apart,
Will dash its torrents, till each soaking sod
Becomes mere clay, a soften'd human heart.

Some day that harp, thrill'd by a hand so strong
That keener mastery would its tension break,
Will feel the chords of hidden music wake,
In one wild, throbbing, passionate love song.

And the swift thoughts that surge within your
    brain,
Like an unerring pendulum will beat
For ever to the stroke which cleft in twain
Your coolest will and left it at white heat.

Ah ! talk not of your power o'er self and love,
Did you but know its force you would be dumb,
'Tis manhood's prime, life's strongest levers move,
With youth's last sighs the days of passion come.

IN THE "TIMES."

"Now for the marriages, births and deaths!
Young Chator, I see, is made a papa,
Tom's tied to his cousin Elizabeth,
And——Here, May! you read these through to
    mamma."

She's dead, then—my lost love of long ago!
Long ago—though it seems as the week gone by
When we sat alone by the river's flow,
And talk'd of the future, my love and I.

But the future with sorrow was rife!
Since love in a cottage was not my plan,
We parted—I chose a wealthier wife,
And she—she married a rich old man.

Some said she never was quite the same.
How well I remember that moonlit scene
When she whisper'd, "George! it is you to blame,
I would have been true, had you been."

Would I had seen her but once again !
Would I could see her ! Ah ! even now,
To tell in those deaf ears my life-long pain,
To press one kiss on that marble brow.

Is she alter'd, I wonder ? have years
Left their trail in her glossy hair ?
Have grief, disappointment, watching and tears,
Spoilt the face that was once so fair ?

My wife has been all a wife can be,
Leal and loving, gentle and true ;
But never the pulse of my life to me
Like her of whose passion *she* never knew.

Eh ! children ?—What ? then my eldest-born
Cries out with reproach in her very tone,
And a tinge of youthful, pitying scorn,
" Papa, you have no more romance than a stone !

" Read this." But my thoughts they are far away ;
I hear my wife say, " There, May, let him be !
Your father is dreaming of settling day,
Or some money-making for you and for me."

Settling day ! yes ! when, beyond the sky,
I meet my dead love as of old we met,
Shall we two speak of the trials gone by,
Or shall we in mercy the past forget?

The clock strikes nine—I rise from my chair,
Straightway all my fanciful visions are furl'd,
I am off to the office—once more to be there
Myself—the keen, shrewd, business man of the
  world.

A COMMON STORY.

A ROSEBUD bloom'd upon a thorny stem,
A virgin veil of moss her sweetness hid,
Like some rare, fragrant, oriental gem,
Peeping from out the casket's fretwork lid.

The sunbeam wooed it with love-lighted smile,
The zephyr sought it in the evening breeze,
The rosebud mourn'd her cruel fate the while,
Not to be sought by higher loves than these.

A lightning flash shot through the summer sky!
"Were that my love!" the ambitious rosebud
    sigh'd,
The lightning heard the impetuous, wishful cry,
And rent the veil of sheltering moss aside.

Quick to the rosebud's heart the wild flash clave,
Only to leave that heart asunder riven,
Her beauty, fragrance, bloom, she gladly gave,
To be forsaken almost ere they're given.

Roses just bursting into balmy prime,
Look down upon her now, with well-bred sneer,
E'en others, faded by the kiss of time,
May safely launch their shafts of slander here.

Within her warm and glowing heart she grieves,
And weeping dew-drop tears in passionate pride,
Wraps herself up within her mournful leaves,
Only too glad the blush of shame to hide.

Fast falls refreshingly a thunder shower,
Charming away the lightning's scorching heat,
Spoiling the bloom of many a flaunting flower,
But to the rosebud's ears 'tis comfort sweet.

Poor rosebud, lift thy stricken, drooping head,
Gaze not on earth, but meekly turn to heaven !
For such as thee, those cooling drops are shed
From there—where only follies are forgiven.

TWO PICTURES.

A HARVEST field and a hedge-row thick
Where the pale wild roses blow,
Where strong men work at the half-thatch'd
    rick,
And the children play below !
Where the crimson glow of the setting sun,
Bathes the hills in floods of light,
And the honest calm of a day's work done,
Is the benison of night !

A battle-field where the bravest fell,
And the ground is strewn with slain ;
Where the death seed sown was the bursting shell,
And the harvest,—shrieks of pain !

Where vultures gloat o'er blood-stain'd success,
And the burden of future years
Is the wailing cry of the fatherless
And the widow's heart-wrung tears.

Say you who mould a nation's story,
Which picture is a statesman's glory ?

NEVER DOUBT IT.

THE chestnut lies in the chestnut rind !
Rough and prickly the bur may be,
There's a sweet, sound nut in the nest behind,
With its velvet lining away from the world.
What does it matter to human-kind,
'Tis white and warm where the nut lies curl'd,
'Tis cosy and soft where no eyes can see.

The pearl lies shut in the oyster shell !
Hard and jagged the shell may be,
But a thousand tints that the sun loves well,
Rich as the rainbow's archway bright,
Softer, smoother than brush can tell,
With all its touches of warmth and light
Cradle the gem where no eyes can see.

A love lies folded within a life !
Stern and rugged the life may be,
First in the din of discord's strife,
There's a quiet spot kept for the love to lie,
Where never an angry cloud is rife,
To cross the blue of the sunlit sky,
'Tis always summer where none can see.

PASSING.

THE days are dying out !
On the old year's hearthstone lie
Just the embers, that is all—
And we watch the quick sparks fly
And the empty ashes fall
    With a sigh !

The years are dying out !
Every one that swiftly goes
Tears a shred of youth and joy ;
But it gives us at its close
Only more of earth's alloy,
    And its woes !

The lives are dying out!
Not a year but some one gone—
Leaves a niche that none can fill.
May God spare our best, our own,
For the world is dark and chill,
All alone!

A REVERIE.

A REVERIE.

I.

IN A JEWELLER'S WINDOW.

ONLY a commonplace thing in itself,
Amongst a heap of commonplace things ;—
A silver Cupid with golden wings,
Wheeling a barrow, along a shelf,
Piled to the full with new wedding rings.
Yet in that barrow an inch across
Lie slavery's fetters, and bonds of bliss,
Infinite gain, infinite loss ;
Tragedies dark as the shades of Dis
Quiet havens where storm clouds cease,
Passion, satiety, war and peace.

II.

A child cries, wearied with its play,
" These toys are all so tame and dumb,
I've play'd with them for half the day,
I wish the lady moon would come,
Or that some twinkling star would fall
With all its rays of glittering light.
Oh ! will they answer if I call ?
And be my playmates for a night ?"

A maiden fresh as spring's first kiss
Or April violets wet with dew,
Sits, dreaming of an unknown bliss,
An unknown life where all is new.
She heeds no tale that parents tell,
Impatient of their care divine,
But cries, " Ah ! all things will be well
When matron dignity is mine."

Pale woman with that wedding ring,
The first link of your slavery's chain,
What now is your imagining ?
Were all your hopes and wishes vain ?

What is the cry of riper years?
And she half murmuring, half aloud,
Replies, " My life is drain'd of tears,
I pray God only for a shroud."

III.

But turn we now to fairer themes,
And in a maiden's love-lit eyes
Read all the thoughts, and hopes, and dreams
Which coming marriage sanctifies.

We watch her through the waning hours
Where maidenhood's soft sunset falls,
And turns each joy to jewell'd flowers
Bright as Aladdin's magic halls.

'Tis the last day of maiden life,
And even now the daylight dies ;
The sun sinks weary of the strife
With darkening clouds and wintry skies.

IV.

They are busy in the household, she is left to rest
    awhile,
Lest to-morrow's white rose pallor steal the lustre
    from her smile ;
Through the echoes rolling sadly, comes the chime
    of bygone years,
And the future answers gladly 'mid her dower of
    smiles and tears.

Childhood's cuckoo pints and daisies, and the scent
    of new-mown hay ;
Every power like buds in spring-time, that are panting
    for the day.

Then the dewy flush of morning, and the hopes half
    understood,
As the dark-fringed lids droop'd shyly 'neath the kiss
    of maidenhood.

Then her thoughts go swiftly forward to the country
    lanes and stiles,
And her laughing lips part lightly in a rippling wave
    of smiles.

Whilst her flush'd cheeks dimple deeply, and the
   twinkling firelight flies
Up to greet its mocking sister, that warm mischief in
   her eyes.

Not with one, but, ah! with many, she has play'd that
   game of love
As the moon now wanes, now waxes, to the changeless
   stars above.

Then a softer shadow follows, and the smiles die out
   again ;
It was half a sigh, that whisper, and the glance was
   almost pain !

For in thought she sees a meeting 'neath the berried
   mountain ash,
And a falling tear lies threaded for a moment on a
   lash.

He had loved her—ay, so fondly—mid the ripening
   harvest sheaves,
'Mid September's waning beauty and the drift of
   falling leaves,

When the red sun lost his power and the summer
　　glory turn'd
To dull tints, while glowing crimson the Virginian
　　creeper burn'd.

He had loved her, ay, so fondly—though the rest
　　might come and go—
It had cost her half a struggle when she sigh'd and
　　said him " No."

All his virtues come before her, all his strength of
　　heart and limb,
Yet her smile breaks through the shadows, he was
　　good !—but, ah !—not *him*.

Then to "*him*" her thoughts flee onward scarce a
　　twelvemonth's span ago,
When the firelight flash'd its welcome through the
　　drizzling sleet and snow ;

When the holly's polish'd scutcheons gleam'd like
　　sconces on the wall,
And the mistletoe's pale berries laugh'd a challenge
　　in the hall,

She knew not *then* the reason she was anxious to look
    fair,
Nor why she bribed the gardener for the rosebud in
    her hair.

What is the mute monition that our guardian angels
    send ?
Why cared she aught that evening for her brother's
    college friend ?

She knew—too well—by Easter, when her quicken'd
    love had burst
Like the daffodil's pale blossoms that the winter
    snows had nursed.

Pale *are* spring-flower gifts of beauty—but the spring-
    tide sun and rain
Bring the summer's wealth of roses, with their passion
    and their pain.

Love has thorns as well as roses, and the tiny weapons
    prick
Like the sting of venom'd arrows to the life-blood's
    soul and quick.

It was on the Easter morning when the dripping
    woods were wet,
And the cold winds scared the fragrance from the
    shrinking violet,

That she knew not how to fathom all the mystery
    of his eyes
Where a softer look stole sometimes like the blue
    athwart the skies.

Cold and damp, and harsh and cheerless, are those
    early days of spring
When the east winds drive the sunshine from the
    earth all shivering.

Cold and harsh and dark and cheerless seem'd her
    life that Easter day,
With the east wind blowing through it, and the sun-
    shine gone astray.

Yet the fresh leaves speak of gladness and the caw-
    ing of the rooks,
And the odour of the meadows and the rushing of the
    brooks,

Shout their one unalter'd story that the reign of
  winter's done,
That the earth waits glad and patient for the coming
  of the sun !

But *her* sun was slow in coming, and faint hope had
  almost died
When the breath of lilacs usher'd the warm kiss of
  Whitsuntide.

Then once more he came to see them, though he
  might not hold her dear,
Yet—(alas ! for girlhood's folly !) it was sweet to have
  him near.

Once more they stroll'd together through the quiet
  garden walks,
By the tall Narcissi vestals on their slim and stately
  stalks.

Past the shrubbery's bright fringes where the guelder
  rose's snow
Fell by every breeze light-lifted on the pansy hearts
  below ;

Where laburnum like a syren shook her locks of
  molten gold,
And Syringa sigh'd the sweetness that her heart's
  too full to hold ;

To the quaint old kitchen garden, with its sunny south-
  west wall,
Where the ripening peaches waited till the summer
  tide should fall ;

And the white-veil'd blossom'd pear-tree dropp'd
  her petals like a bride,
Who, impatient of her finery, throws her wedding
  robes aside.

They loiter'd by espaliers, and the flushing beauty
  told
Of the russet wealth of autumn the full-fruited boughs
  would hold.

Then he pluck'd a knot of wallflowers, and the
  fragrant gold and brown
Lent a charm of quiet beauty to the bosom of her
  gown.

And they talk'd of buds and blossoms, of the spring-
    time and the bees,
Of the swallows lightly skimming; though their
    thoughts were not with these.

It was underneath the lime trees—whilst a chaffinch
    piped o'erhead,
That his arm stole gently round her, and those few
    brief words were said :—

Said ! nay, half-express'd and whisper'd, and her
    faltering, low reply,
Like the pear-tree's fluttering petals which the west
    wind drifted by.

" I have loved you, sweet, since Christmas, but I
    dared not speak before,
I thought you cared just for me—as your brother's
    friend—no more."

" And I've long'd and waited for you." " Ah ! my
    love, had I but guess'd—"
Then in silence died the sentence, as her head droop'd
    on his breast.

Ah ! who cares to break such silence ? words are part
    of this world's leaven,
There are moments in a lifetime when the earth just
    touches heaven.

We can only wait uplifted—but a word—a sigh, a
    sign,
And again the chasm's yawning 'twixt the human
    and divine.

    *   *   *   *   *

Then that warm love-hallow'd summer, when the
    very roses wore
A richer garb of beauty than they ever knew be-
    fore ;
When bliss lurk'd in every sunbeam, in each bud and
    blossom curl'd,
Till the wondrous haze of glory made an Eden of
    the world.

So sped the fleet months onward, and the year brought
    all too soon
October's dreamy softness and the mellow harvest
    moon,

When he pleaded for an answer ere he left for town
    again,
For the wedding-day decided ere the moon was on
    the wane.

For three long days she waited—saying neither yea
    nor nay,
" The harvest moon is full yet, Love, have patience
    for a day."

Half withholding and half giving, just a word retracted
    soon—
Till patience reach'd its limits like the full of harvest
    moon :

And he swore the truce was over : when that evening
    kiss'd the day—
From his arms he would not loose her, till she gave
    him all his way.

It was by the shrubbery border where the hollyhocks
    once blew,
And their sodden stems hung limply in the rising fog
    and dew ;

Where amid the damp leaf odour came a fragrance
 even yet
From heliotrope fast dying, and the fainting mignonette.

Sigh'd the south wind softly by them, as through
 laurel boughs and bays
She linger'd searching sadly for the long lost summer
 days.

Chirp'd the robin winter's welcome—fell the yellow
 leaves in showers
As they drifted sad and tearful to the burial of the
 flowers.

Stream'd the glorious moonlight calmly from the deep
 blue vault above,
Like the grief of mortals soften'd by the heaven-sent
 gift of love.

Silent stood she, coy and wilful, with her eyes bent
 on the ground,
And her pulses beating wildly with his prisoning arms
 around.

Silent stood she, heeding nothing of his wild, dis-
  jointed talk,
Whilst one little heel ground slowly on the spongy
  garden walk.

Silent stood she, coy and wilful, crimson cheeks and
  downcast eyes,
Then she pleaded it was " sudden," she was " taken
  by surprise."

But the coyest lips love kisses—and the shyest maiden's
  frown
Is a cobweb floating idly, where Love breaks the
  barriers down.

Still for man is sweet beseeching—still 'tis woman's
  to deny,
Yet the varying notes are wedded in an endless
  harmony.

     *   *   *   *

Ah! the past has been so happy! as she leans back
  in her chair,
She weaves a thousand castles in the shadowy world
  of air.

Like a spectre passing through them comes the
    thought of other lives,
Where Time has brought dark changes both to
    husbands and to wives.

Will *their* love fade into liking as the years roll on
    apace,
And they reach the dull, dead level of the hopeless
    commonplace ;

Though united, yet divided ; though together, yet
    alone ;
With love's tenderest accents sinking to one dreary
    monotone ?

Nay ! a happier fate awaits them, where the glory
    and the glow
Of early wedlock passion through the gathering years
    will grow ;

Where the grindstone of existence, and the sharpest
    cares of life,
Will but make more closely fitting hearts of husband
    and of wife.

Then she weaves a quiet picture of the joys of house
    and home,
Of life for ever with him, and the years of love to
    come.

Till wearied by excitement, thoughts of past and
    present cease,
And the hollow cinders falling add a warm Amen of
    peace.

Weird, half ghostly, half fantastic, steal the shadows
    o'er the wall,
And the quicken'd firelight leaping throws its ruddy
    glow o'er all.

Then the phantom dustman enters, o'er her lids his
    fingers creep,
With a sigh of soft contentment she is gently hush'd
    asleep.

She is tired and sleeps soundly, for no thrill her
    pulses stir,
Though her mother stands beside her, and a dearer
    still with her.

V.

Hush! the winter twilight closes,
And the firelight's flickering glare
Shows a sweeter pair of roses
Than the summer's sweetest were.
See, my darling! is aught fairer?
Of my treasure envious grown,
(Asking not if I could spare her),
Sleep has claim'd her for his own.

Hush! be still; I would not waken,
Save by one long, lingering kiss,
Such pure loveliness, o'ertaken
By a slumber sweet as this.
How the mocking firelight flashes
In short, fitful gleams of light,
On her curling, silken lashes,
On her blue-vein'd eyelids white.

On her red lips, softly parted,
On her smooth, broad, thoughtful brow;
Never bosom truer-hearted
Beat on earth than beats there now.

I could gaze on her for ever!
Ah! I pause, and hold my breath,
Surely, frailest bars must sever
Kindly sleep from cruel death.

Oh! that thought! Like chill dews creeping,
Myriad fears come trooping past,
Darling! wake! if 'tis but sleeping,
Wake! 'tis I who hold you fast.
See! she smiles, my glad heart bounding,
Breathes a prayer not loud but deep,
May the last trump's awful sounding
Be Love's summons out of sleep!

VI.

Keenly blows the wintry wind!
Cold the starlight gleams above!
What is cold to lover-kind?
Where's the blast that chilleth love?

Sweetliest sweet of all farewells!
Scarce a farewell counted this,
When the glad full-throated bells
Shout she is for ever his!

Shy and wistful is her face,
Coy lips utter not a word,
Folded in that close embrace,
All her very soul is stirr'd.

Full content o'ermasters will,
Silently she nestles there,
Lets him strain her closer still,
Kiss her lips and eyes and hair.

Hark! her sisters' voices call!
" One more kiss, *one* more, my own."
Then she glides within the hall,
And he leaves the house alone.

When he next shall leave that door,
In the sunshine or the snow,
She'll be with him evermore,
Side by side for weal or woe.

VII.

In the old house every rafter
Gleams with warmth and cheerful light,
Rings to girls' low silvery laughter,
Let each one be glad to-night.

With *her* merriment is mingled
Just that shade of pensive thought,
As from lilies one is singled
By the shadow it has caught.

Not the thunder-cloud of sorrow,
But the evening's golden haze,
Which foretells upon the morrow
Sunniest of sunny days.

VIII.

Night's soft silence stills the laughter,
On the stairs the echoes die,
Yet she watches long, long after
Sleep has folded every eye.

Watches with her heart yet thrilling
To her mother's fond Good-night,
Half reluctant and half willing
For the dawn of morning light.

As the moon has slowly broken
From the night clouds' dark eclipse,
So the thoughts as yet unspoken,
Part the words upon her lips.

Words as pure as angel's blessing,
Or the prayer that gives them birth,
All the hidden hopes confessing
That she cannot breathe to earth.

IX.

'Tis nearly midnight ! and the hours to come
No human power can retard or stay,
To-morrow brings new life—new love—new home,
To-morrow's dawning brings my wedding day !
Yes, mine, God help me ! Would I fain turn back ?
No, for *this* time all fears and struggles cease.
Some thorns may hide amid the future's track,
But Love's soft fingers strew its path with peace.

And all those dreams and loves of long ago
Fade, as the starlight fades before the sun,
A memory, not a shadow ; for I know
There is but *one* by whom my heart was won.
And the last whispers of my maiden life
Are voiceless prayers, that I may ever be
All that he loves and longs for in a wife.
Ay ! and I trust him, he'll not change to me !

" I have no fears, not one ; I know each heart
Is but the echo of the other's beat.
I *know* our lives, no longer lived apart,
Will join, as join two rivers when they meet.
Father ! by Whom all precious gifts are sent,
I ask but one more boon this night from Thee,
To crown the blessedness of glad content,
Grant that *our* life may be one lived for Thee."

X.

Gleaming through the darkness comes a flush of
    red,
Falling like soft blushes round her maiden bed,
Timid daylight enters as the wan clouds part,
Rolling back their ermine from the sun king's
    heart.

'Tis the wedding morning ! quickly, sweet, arise,
For the sun is shining in the cold grey skies ;
Happy brides are shone on, happy, then, are you,
Waiting for the bridal, husband fond and true.

Nay, lips must not falter, courage must not fail
'Neath the orange blossoms and the filmy veil ;
Make her look her fairest, each expectant eye
Lights with eager interest as the bride goes by.

XI.

Holy, mystic Trinity,
Three in One, and One in Three,
Perfect Love and Purity:

Bless these two now kneeling here,
Guide them in Thy faith and fear,
Each to each the more endear.

Bless this awful marriage oath,
Wedded hearts and plighted troth,
Let the tie lie light on both.

Sorrow, sickness, need or pain,
Worldly loss or worldly gain,
Be but fresh links in the chain.

Whatsoever ills befall,
Each to each be all in all,
Love give honey with the gall.

Whatsoever fate betide,
Howsoever toss'd and tried,
Never, Lord, to leave Thy side.

Till their wedded love shall be
Perfect in its unity,
One themselves, and one with Thee.

XII.

Throw the hall door open wide !
For the carriage-wheels are heard.
" Wish you joy, *Ma'am !*" to the bride,
How she blushes at the word !

Lead her through the open door
To the study, nothing loth :
" One sweet, fond embrace before
All the guests are round us both."

First she blushes, then turns pale,
Shrinking from this strange new life,
As her husband lifts her veil,
Calls her by the name of wife.

Cold the ring yet on her hand,
For those slight, slim fingers slack,
Yet she feels its iron band,
Knows there is no turning back.

Is she sorry? is she glad?
What a rising tumult stirs
Thoughts half joyful and half sad,
In that struggling heart of hers.

Little time has she to think,
Carriage after carriage rolls,
Flirt, cry, chatter, eat and drink,
Feast of reason! flow of souls!

XIII.

Take the flowers from her hair,
Heed not all those gathering tears,
Cheer her, say she must look fair
When the bridegroom's voice she hears.

Never heed her ! talk away,
Sharp is this last parting hour,
Partings on a bridal day
Are the thorns upon the flower.

Bridesmaids, do your very best,
Ah ! her mother breaks her down,
Let her sob, that mother's breast
Bore the cross, this is her crown.

Let her sob ! Love copes with love,
Strongest weapons aye must win,
Childhood's home is but a glove
Shielding the warm hand within.

Nature's voice is strong and clear,
Every hand must soon or late
Grasp its nettle without fear,
By itself decide its fate.

XIV.

The honeymoon's languorous days are past !
Pass'd all their feverish heat and glow,
They stand together, their two lots cast
In earnest now, for Life's weal and woe.

Softly the coming days may flit,
Softly the moon may wax and wane,
But never shine on those fond eyes lit
With young Love's rapture and bliss again.

The down is brush'd from the gather'd fruit,
The delicate gossamer sails are furl'd,
Another passion must now take root,
And Love wake up in a fresh new world ;

A world where lingers no glamour nor mist,
No wandering sunbeam of Youth's ideal,
But clear-cut Practice, whose soul and gist
Is sense and management, hard and real.

And they, with their life like a flask whose seal
Is crisp, new rosin, which cracks and fails,
As o'er the threshold their footsteps steal,
And Home's first shelter a welcome calls,

What will they do with their unseal'd life,
That life they challenged in eager haste ?
Have patience, husband, and young bride wife,
Those first few drops have a bitter taste !

The deep-lipp'd chalice with tears is wet,
Trials cost some struggles, however fond,
Two souls strange clashing of will—and yet
The draught *is* honey, below, beyond.

Fear not the future, because of now,
Nor spill its sweetness in swift disgust,
Let patience follow your bridal vow,
Her meek hands laden with hope and trust.

Then through the silence shy Peace will steal,
To fling her roses beneath your feet,
To kiss the chalice, until you feel
The deep full charm of Life's bitter-sweet :

And link'd in bonds, that to young Love's chain
Of spangled cobweb are gold to sand,
You'll learn this lesson, no longer twain,
But one for aye—till the shadow land.

Break not the fetters around you cast !
That flask of honey is full and deep ;
Time strokes the eyes of the childish past,
Till childlike, weary, 'tis hush'd asleep.

And strong life wakes up to touch and sight
As the young Phœnix waking flies
Forth from the ashes, still half alight
Where a yet beauteous Phœnix dies!

Believe them not, who call wedlock's gold
Mere apples dropp'd in an eager chase,
Mere chance-found treasures, both hard and cold,
Soon merged in cares of the commonplace.

The draught God gives for true hearts to drink
Has no chance sweetness, no measured mean,
No trials, no troubles, no moneyed chink,
Can cloud or poison or come between.

'Tis seal'd-up treasure, and that is all!
It needs more seeking than moonlit dreams,
Some sighs may herald, some tears may fall,
Then bright as Heaven its beauty gleams.

XV.

A look! ay, it is half a frown!
A word! at which Love frighten'd flies!
The same event to both sent down,
But view'd by different pairs of eyes.

A half-way step advanced by each,
A few soft words, as arms steal round,
And lost in kisses farther speech,
What sweeter kisses can be found ?

And so the argument is done,
As summer clouds, surcharged with rain,
Just dim the brightness of the sun,
With drops his warmth will woo again ;

To live for ever at noonday,
Would blind our eyes with garish light,
Far sweeter shines each morning ray,
When fresh from the repose of night.

And even love might cloy with bliss,
If all were bliss, without a shade,
Life's richest rhythm we should miss,
If endless harmony it made.

It is but Love, which dares to make
A discord in that perfect strain,
In unskill'd hands the harp-strings break,
And never breathe of love again ;

So artist's brush with magic skill
Some wondrous loveliness portrays,
But lest bright tints with brightness kill,
Adds one soft touch of chasten'd greys.

XVI.

The theory that each woman heart
Holds blended with its very blood
Fountains of love and bliss, which start
At the mere thought of motherhood :

How false it is ! Far heavier lot
Falls on most women, pain and fear,
And patient waiting, knowing not
The issue of the cross they bear.

And mother-love in many a one
Is closed as fast as buds in spring,
Which open shuddering to the sun
After a winter's suffering ;

With every pang a leaf unroll'd,
Till the sweet dewy heart uncurls,
And the awaken'd arms enfold
A new Cornelia's string of pearls.

She thinks perhaps it may be sweet
To hear amid fast gliding years
The patter of two tiny feet,
A child's light laughter 'midst its tears ;

But will she hear it ?   Once again
Her heart half stops : then beats aloud ;
Love's awful sacrifice of pain
Lays many a mother in her shroud :

When spring comes softly round the hill,
With violets nestled in her breast,
Will she be lying cold and still,
In long unbroken, dreamless rest ?

And he ? her dearest one—her own,
Seek home and find no comfort there,
But sorrow's dreary monotone,
A missing voice—an empty chair ?

And then he comes and dries her tears,
Though his own heart is sick with dread,
And tells her, these are common fears,
Mere details of her state, 'tis said.

Till soothed and comforted ere long
The room with mellow laughter rings ;
And crooning low a wistful song,
She plies her needle as she sings.

XVII.

How came Baby here ?
Under the hedgerow a violet grew,
Meekly to heaven its soft eye look'd up,
Wildly and fiercely the keen March winds blew,
One little tear-drop of heaven-sent dew
Fell in the heart of that pure chalice cup.
Then angel fingers just gather'd the whole,
Sweet baby violet ! God-given soul !

How came Baby here ?
All in the hush and the silence of night,
One little star trembled out in the sky,
Shone with a steadfast, unwavering light,
Clear as the day, as a diamond bright,
God smiled upon it, and bless'd it on high.
Hark ! through the silence the angels' songs roll,
Sweet little baby star ! God-given soul !

How came Baby here?
Once up to heaven there floated a prayer,
'Twas but the spirit of Love in a sigh,
So its own purity wafted it where
That life is born, which can never more die.
Then softly down with the angels it stole,
Sweet little baby star !   God-given soul.

XVIII.

But weary months have come and gone,
And still her steps are weak and slow,
The pear-trees' blossoms and the thorn
Shed all their beauty long ago :

The buttercups are in the grass,
The nightingales have ceased to sing,
The languid days of summer pass,
But leave her weaker than the spring.

And yet through all—through hours of pain,
Through days of dreariness and gloom.
His love and patience never wane ;
Regret's grey thistles cannot bloom !

And when the sun has tann'd the wheat
And crept into the filberts' core,
Health comes to her with truant feet,
And she's his own bright wife once more !

XIX.

I must pause, though fain I'd follow through each
varying mood and state,
These dream children of my fancy, who flit towards
the ivory gate ;

" Towards the ivory gate ! Ah ! never," on the breath
of Truth is borne,
" Such a dream as you have vision'd passes through
the gate of horn."

Yea, I know, and thank God for it ! though the
world may doubt or sneer,
In a million homes this moment, wedlock's torch
burns bright and clear ;

And my own reflects their radiance : in the memories
of the Past,
In the sweetness of the Present, in the love around
me cast,

I can flash back answering brightness, and can pray
   the Powers divine
To send down to lives true-hearted all the love that
   hallows mine!

XX.

Time turns his hour-glass again, dear heart!
And slowly dropping down his grains of gold,
Another year's full freight of joy and smart
   Is past and told.

God bless the day that we two, darling, met!
Our guardian angels wrote the date above,
And won your wife the truest heart that yet
   Bless'd woman's love!

Our married life is now no longer new,
Nor are we novices in wedlock's race;
We've reach'd the goal (if what they say is true)
   Of commonplace!

Yet in our life we see no fading hues,
Amid our love we see no worn-out strands;
Had we our choice in wedlock, still we'd choose
   The self-same bands.

The soft love rays which warm'd love's early life
Still throw a glamour o'er each eve and morn,
The rosy chains of husband and of wife
    Are lightly worn.

And with the every-day of care and work
The golden radiance of pure joy is blent,
Till in their heaviest, darkest shadows,
    Peace and content.

And even tear-drops glisten in its light,
As dewdrops glitter on an autumn day :
The garish summer, with its sunshine bright,
    Has pass'd away.

But in the cool and temper'd autumn sun
The full grapes yield their soul of love and wine ;
So our lives blended, welded into one,
    Yield love divine.

And through all blessings of our wedlock oath,
And through its troubles and its cares we pray
One changeless prayer, " Our Father, take us both
    The self-same day."

THROUGH THE FURNACE.

MESSAGES.

TAKE me the closer in thine arms, my own,
Since o'er Life's path the shades of evening creep,
Ah! 'twill be dreary for you all alone
    When I am hush'd asleep.

Yet, oh! my darling, do not idly fret,
So much remains for you to plan and do,
A few poor things I ask—do not forget
    Those few I ask of you.

Forget! ay me! 'tis I who now forget,
Forgive me, dear! I grow so faint and weak ;
When did request escape your memory yet,
    That I have cared to speak?

So when my weariness is hush'd to rest,
In the first calm of those still, quiet hours,
Let all come here of those who loved me best,
    And cover me with flowers ;

Frail maiden-hair and blossoms white as snow.
I shall look down from my bright home above,
And feel they loved me well, and they—they know
    I gave back love for love.

Say to the few I've wrong'd, if such there be,
" She pray'd forgiveness for each stone she cast."
I never injured aught intentionally,
    Hot words are soonest past.

And say to those fresh girls who wavering stand,
Some eager, some half shrinking, some unstirr'd,
On the dim entrance of that border-land
    Where Life's first call is heard :

Say to them, they who listen'd to my voice,
As soldiers listen to a bugle call,
I leave to them a legacy—a choice
    Of all that may befall.

Tell them that love is sweetest of the sweet,
One ray of Heaven, unwavering and clear,
But they who thrill—ay, to their heart's best beat
    Find many a trouble near.

Tell them that love can brighten every loss,
Tell them that love is God's own sunshine shed
Upon the lichens of a world-worn cross,
    From the blue skies o'erhead.

But tell them, too, that sweet as love is sweet,
Is *work*—the power to plan, and dare, and do ;
That work undone, no life can be complete,
    No soul be wholly true.

Tell them that love alone—is but a pool
Of stagnant water, where all life must die ;
That work should float upon its bosom cool,
    Like water lilies lie.

Tell them thus only happiness is won ;
That though I fainted 'neath my own bless'd creed,
Yet in these last few hours when all is done,
    I feel it bless'd indeed.

And tell them one thing else—that more than love,
And more than work—though work and love are one,
Is the sweet faith He gives us from above
    In Him—our Life's true Sun.

And guide our daughter wisely ; self-will'd, proud,
Quick, passionate, she shares her mother's curse,
Still to be one, where others are a crowd,
    But, dear, it might be worse.

So guide her wisely, do not spoil nor spare,
Through over-tenderness, that opening life,
For firm control must lay her blessing where
    Such keen self-will is rife.

And such as she must be the worst or best ;
God help me ! I've not been, I'd hardly time ;
And yet may-be 'tis better to find rest
    Ere one has reach'd one's prime.

Now, darling, listen, for what next I say,
I whisper from my soul to only you,
And from my very soul of souls I pray,
    It bear fruit full and true.

When you are past the first great sense of loss
Let new-born hope awake within your life,
Let soft hands wreathe fair flowers about your cross,
    And woo another wife.

You cannot, will not, well then let it be!
Press me the closer in those arms of thine,
I ask no promises,—but think of me,
    If brighter days should shine.

Dear heart, I cannot talk, nor could words tell
Your tenderness, your goodness, dear, good-bye!
That which the Master sends us, it is well,
    I am content to die.

Ah! not content to leave you; oh! my own,
My life's best pulse, keep back those blinding tears,
Think how the past on lightning wings has flown,
    They'll pass, these parted years.

Oh! do not grieve so, looking at your face,
It makes me all unfitted for the strife,
Fold me the closer in that fond embrace,
    Pray God to spare your wife!

EXISTENCE.

A DRIFTING boat down a sleepy stream,
With the current choked by the tangled grass,
Where the night mists rise like a fever'd dream,
And only the will-o'-wisp's empty gleam
Through the gathering gloom of their darkness pass.

And evermore with the voice of care
There blends the cry of that long ago,
When the stream ran clear and the skies were fair,
And the long grass waved in the summer air,
And hope was *real*, not delusive show.

Is it a dream ? but a passing thrill,
An empty flutter of fancy's wings,
That once my life was a sparkling rill,
Which turn'd full many a water mill,
And fed the grass whence the skylark springs ?

Ay ! it *was so !* with a wail of pain,
The truth in its cruel frankness calls,
It was so, never to be again,
For the lights are false and the hopes are vain,
And o'er the future grim darkness falls.

Ay, bitter darkness ! yet overhead
A star shines out in the quiet sky,
The path is hard that my tired feet tread,
But the one soft gleam from the starlight shed,
Speaks comfort, hope, in the by-and-bye.

HOPE.

OH ! weary hope !
Hope that so catches at the skirts of fear,
That her shy footsteps are but faintly heard
Beneath his heavy tread, whose echo drear
Strikes the heart cold as by a cruel word.

Oh ! weary hope !
Hope, that so lags upon the path of life,
Her coming is but sorrow in disguise ;
Her smiles as dangerous as the storm-cloud rife
Within the east wind treachery of spring skies.

Oh ! weary hope !
Hope that is wedded surely to despair,
And wears, instead of young corn's ripening ears,
The yew and cypress in her faded hair,
Fit garland for her ministry of tears.

Oh! weary hope!
That with a careless look and mocking jest,
Can bid calm resignation turn and flee,
Then torture with wild, quivering unrest,
The feeble strength that dares to trust in thee.

DISCIPLINE.

STROKE fell on stroke till the anvil rang,
And far and near through the mighty clang
The hot sparks flew, like the stars set free,
Or quick souls bound for Eternity.
Ay, harder yet, with a strength and will,
Fall crushing blows 'mid the clang and thrill.
'Twould beat to atoms less sturdy stuff,
That seething iron is strong enough!
It gleams and falters beneath each blow,
Whilst swifter, hotter, the red sparks glow,
Till beaten, bruised into fainting strength,
It lies stretched out in its rugged length—
A rough-hewn mass out of anguish hurl'd,
A lever now that could move a world.

   *   *   *   *   *   *

Thus fall the blows with a clang and thrill
On heart's deep passions and brain's strong will ;
Thus lives are crush'd whilst their hopes fly fast,
And the glad, hot days of youth's prime are past.
Ay, harder yet—in each thrill and clang,
Each cruel trial, each killing pang,
Is born one shred of keen self-control,
Of quiet patience and strength of soul,
Till out of the quickening fire is hurl'd
The giant strength which can move a world.

REST.

WHEN, with a cross too hard to bear,
We faint beneath its weight at length,
Lean but the more upon His strength,
And patience is itself a prayer :

A prayer, that, flying like a dove,
High o'er the floods of sin and grief,
Brings back with it an olive-leaf
Of quicken'd faith and trusting love.

And though the hopes which throng'd our path
Like feather'd nestlings take to wing,
Yet, soaring up to Heaven, they sing
Of skies unstirr'd by tempest's wrath.

Hush'd is the anxious, quivering pain,
The eager plans and wild unrest ;
We feel He surely knoweth best—
His hands will wind the tangled skein !

Then, with God's blessing over all,
The quiet, peaceful days unfold
Like roses, with their hearts of gold
Shown most when half the petals fall.

And that soft calm when struggles cease,
Falls like the dew on fever'd life ;
Without—the rush and toil and strife ;
Within—the heaven-sent gift of peace.

Perchance hereafter (when these years,
Through mists of cloudy memories, gleam
Like some weird, half-forgotten dream)
We'll thank Him less for joy than tears.

COMPENSATION.

HARD was my lot and bitter!   None can tell
The weariness of all that time of gloom!
Youth's brightest hopes shut in a prison cell;
Life's fairest years pass'd in a dull sick-room.

*   *   *   *   *

Then Love stepp'd softly—never music made
A sweeter echo than his gentle tread—
And whispering, " *My* joys can never fade,"
He hung a wreath of roses o'er my bed.

Then Friendship caught my hand with kindling
      eyes,
Her zone of glittering starlight wide unfurl'd;
Far more than heart can count I found my prize
Each separate star, a warm, bright, human world.

Then Gratitude, with tearful eyes, arose,
And said, in words that brought the tears to mine,
" My prayers go up; from morn till evening's close
A lamp for ever burns before the shrine!"

And Sympathy's unmeasured bounty fell
Thick as the hedge-row's blossom in the spring,
Till through the darkness of my prison cell
The daylight stream'd and birds began to sing.

Then, 'mid the fluttering of unseen wings,
Faith's golden cross shone out, no longer dim,
From whence for ever radiant comfort springs
Like the glad chorus of an Easter hymn.

*   *   *   *   *

Hard is my lot and bitter!   Ay, but Time's
Rough hand crush'd sweetness from that bitter core ;
The very moments ring in silver chimes,
" You never knew you were so loved before."

And ye who suffer, listen,—in my cell
Weeks pass to months, and months glide into years ;
The harrow pass'd, and then the raindrops fell,
But golden is the harvest of full ears.

ΖΩΝΗ ΜΑΡΓΑΡΙΤΩΝ.

Ζωνη μαργαριτων.

A.

Like priceless girdle, wrought with many a gem,
So 'mid the jewels of affection shine
Some clearer than the rest—whose lustre fine
Adds to the less, yet not detracts from them.

Thus, 'mid the many whom I know and prize,
Gleam out the pearls set deep within my soul.
Yet lesser links are needed for a whole,
And 'neath Time's footsteps other gems arise.

So that he adds, but never takes away;
The more the links the better to that chain,
Whose beauty will through coming years remain,
Though cheek grows faded, and though hair is
    grey.

B.

Comely, cosy, dainty Mother,
   Flirting with old Time,
Till he treats you like another,
   Scarcely past her prime.
Looking at you, who'd discover,
   'Mid your folds of lace,
All the years which, passing over,
   Scarcely left a trace.

One year shone for me the clearest,
   When your brown-eyed lad
Came in time to make the dearest
   Husband wife e'er had ;
For though lovers wooed in plenty,
   Gold and Fame and Rank ;
Though I'd listen, ay ! to twenty,
   I loved only Frank.

So, despite the word of omen,
   Keeping most in awe,
Name of dread to many women,
   Mother—but in law,

Take the love your daughter sends you!
All that is your due ;
Some the love *his* loving lends you,
Some just love for you !

Γ.

My gentle cousin, with the quiet eyes,
And manners softer than the cygnet's down,
Who count the joys of home your life's best
    prize,
And children jewels in your wifehood's crown :
Time's wings in flying waft our lives apart,
But his weird pinions only fan the glow
Of byegone thoughts, which thrill within my heart
Like robins piping through the winter snow.

For happy memories of girlhood stream,
Like motes on sunshine, with my thoughts of
    you,
And fluttering souls of many a long-lost dream,
Crowd round my path, and live their lives anew.
I shut my eyes, and youth flies back again ;
I scent the briny odour of the sea ;

I hear the plashing of the soft, spring rain,
And past and present are as one to me!

And those you love I love ; like twisted strands
In one affection many threads combine,
And throw their tendrils, strong as iron bands,
From every blossom of your dear home vine.
There is not *one* that, in the days of old,
Caught my heart's love in that unyielding mesh
But holds it still, like stores of tarnish'd gold,
Needing but friction to be new and fresh.

Δ.

How shall I paint her!   With her silvery hair,
Time's crown of beauty for a life well spent,
And the glad blessedness of sweet content,
Like evening sunshine making all things fair ?
Or dwell on willingness to plan and *do*,
The spirit that to rule is nothing loth ?
Ay, both together, make the portrait true,
And we who love her, love her best as both.

For if the tongue be sharp, the heart is sound ;

A trusty blade has ever keenest edge ;

A rock so firm we trust its slightest ledge,

Is no soft pathway like the swampy ground.

And we who've tried her touch in pain or sorrow,

Her sympathy when all the world look'd cold,

Know guardian angels might their kindness borrow

That ! for mere words, when deeds are wrought in gold!

Dress her in rich brocade and costly lace,

They suit the beauty of her sixty years ;

But lay warm kisses softly on the face

That in its kindly wrinkles shows the trace

Of all her sympathy with others' tears !

E.

Right heavy is the burden laid upon

Her two frail shoulders, but her thin face wears

The lines of suffering where faith has shone,

And turn'd to glory all the cross she bears.

No pining invalid ; with willing hands,

Far-seeing judgment, and clear, active brain,

She turns to good account Time's leaden sands,

And every talent yields its fruit again.

Till on her life—like altar set apart
Where sacrifice and suffering needs must be ;
There falls the love of many a grateful heart,
The censer's incense of sweet charity.

And though four walls her every hope have
    bounded,
Though earthly joys lie in one sad, sick room,
Her Master's voice has through the prison
    sounded,
And bade His rod with almond-blossom bloom.

Z.

Through late September's misty veil
There shines a planet calm and clear,
Whilst twinkling stars gleam far and near ;
And slowly rising o'er the hill,
The harvest crescent, dim and pale,
Hangs like a spectre vague and chill,
Where bounteous fields of grain are shorn
Of all the glory of the corn.

And standing 'mid the ripen'd ears,
I see once more the trusted friend,
Who, through the mist of twenty years
Has loved me still, through smiles, through tears,
And will not falter to the end.
   *   *   *   *   *   *
Mary! I sing no song to you!
That ripen'd corn and full-ear'd sheaves
Are not so precious, nor so true
As memories, neither faint nor few,
Which on my heart our friendship leaves!
Through life's fresh hopes of leafy June,
Through summer's toil and hot success;
Through dim, calm hours of harvest moon,
Through winter's mirth and cheeriness;
There is no scene, but thoughts rise soon
Of all your faith and tenderness.

No wondrous brilliancy of light,
No feverish glare nor sunset glow;
But, like the quiet of the night,
To wearied brain and dazzled sight,
Come all those thoughts of long ago.

II.

Was there a will which ever ruled my own ?
I think so.   Looking back to days gone by,
I catch the accent of a firm, kind tone,
I meet the glance of an unswerving eye—
That conquer'd me—I know not how nor why.

And yet I loved her !   Time and change roll on.
The   world's   experience   chills   fresh   childhood's
    glow,
The sunrise glory from the hills has gone,
And girlish innocence seems years ago—
But she is anchor'd all Life's waves below.

The tares and wheat have both together grown,
Mistakes I reckon by each pulse's beat,
But something else the gathering years have shown—
Successes :—Ay, I lay them at *her* feet,
For 'twas a truth she taught me ere to-day,
They who would rule must first learn to obey.

Θ.

Through the cool primrose-paths of dewy youth,
The soft moss-walks, with early freshness wet,
Where childish innocence and childish truth,
Like mists of morning hang all cloudy yet,
Come faces three, that flit across my mind
Without one shadow of regret or pain :—
Three faces,—each so fresh, so fair, so kind,
They seem like childhood borne to me again.

And, as life's path grows broader, still they stay
With brightest hours of joy and hope and love,
The scent of the roses and the new-mown hay,
And days as cloudless as blue skies above ;
With the soft silence of the moon's pale light,
When common things look strangely, weirdly sweet,
And the soul trembles in the new delight
Of that hush'd spell which makes the pulses beat.

What fairer garland could a poet weave
Around old memories, old friends, than this ?
Spring's freshest morning, golden summer's eve,
A wealth of roses, and true love's first kiss,

K

And moonlit walks where trembling passion's bliss
Thrills now as keenly as when love was new—
Is there one chord that happiness can miss
In that soft harmony which breathes of you ?

I.

Brown eyes (so like another's, even dearer,
Which always hold a loving glance for me)
And kindly lips, which utter no words clearer
Than those of truth and sweet sincerity !
Among new marriage-ties the cordial greeting,
The loveliest matron face I ever met,
Won me, and crown'd you at our earliest meeting
My very pearl of sisters, Margaret.

Since then, time's hour-glass, shifting in his fingers,
Has dropp'd a touch of silver here and there,
And round the honest, genial eyes there lingers
The harrowing line of many an anxious care ;
But liking into loving long has blossom'd.
Let youth go by, nor lose it with regret,
Whilst that warm heart, still in its shrine embosom'd,
Can win us all to you, my Margaret.

Not merely yours the gift of fleeting beauty,
For matron graces grow with growing years,
I deem you fairest 'mid each household duty,
Where hospitality each charm endears.
The mistress of a home whence welcome flashes
Like a clear lamp within the casement set ;
Mere show's cold glitter, covering dust and ashes,
Suits not my pearl of sisters, Margaret.

K.

Fast rolls the Neckar by the terraced walk
Built for that English bride of long ago—
In fancy, still we linger there and talk,
In the soft glamour of a sunset-glow.

In fancy, still I see the tendrill'd vine
Its teeming clusters trail for miles along,
And on the bosom of the storied Rhine,
We breathe the air of legend and of song.

In fancy, still I see a lordly pile,
And gaze with awe upon that wondrous plan,
Whose slender columns and whose glorious aisle
Were surely never traced by mortal man.

Of martyr'd virgins many a crumbling bone,
The wise men's skulls enrich'd by many a gem,
The scents and savours of old-world Cologne—
And thoughts of you are mix'd with thoughts ɔ
      them.

Alas! my friend, that minor chords must come,
The peal of memory rings a muffled chime ;
For some then with us have been summon'd home,
A longer journey than that pleasant time.

A.

Sweet little windflower with the fair, bright face,
And bloom as delicate as Spring's first child,
So soft, so winsome when you blush'd and smiled,
And every movement full of simple grace ;

You and your mother took my heart by storm—
A violet nestling underneath a hedge,
A coy forget-me-not behind the sedge
Of noble bulrushes with princely form.

Which the most precious, sweet one—you or she ?
You, the slight hop in graceful clusters flung,
The prettiest sight your Kentish hills among ;
She, the grand presence of some stately tree,

Or the calm harvest of the golden sheaves,
The quiet woodland nest, where deep peace lies ;
You, the white lilies opening to the skies,
Where dew stays longest on the sheltering
    leaves.

Which the most precious, sweet one—you or
    she ?
I do not know ; I took you both together,
'Mid " traveller's joy " and perfect autumn weather,
Warm welcome and true hospitality.

M.

Of middle height and buxom frame,
    With frank, good-humour'd, laughing eyes,
She looks the picture of her name,
    A naughty Nell in good disguise.

Brown hair just loosely twisted round,
Or brush'd up, without pains or care ;
A finer face was never crown'd
By wisps of more untidy hair.

A pleasant voice, that strikes the ear
Like lithe-wing'd swallow's welcome song,
Which tells of genial summer near,
When frost-nipp'd spring has tarried long.

Care treats her lightly, and old Time
Just chuck'd her 'neath her comely chin,
And left a woman in her prime,
For girlhood's eve to usher in.

Her nature's one grand, royal charm
Is broad-soul'd honour, clear and bright,
Which knows no envious wish to harm,
No petty jealousy nor spite.

Temper she has—the keenest blade
Will surely leave its sign and mark ;
But battle will be fairly made,
No coward's dagger in the dark.

Ζωὴ μαργαριτων.

As independent as the sun,
Her heart is like a hazel-nut,
Rough-husk'd, close-shell'd to every one,
Within its fortress closely shut.

But burst the husk, and break the shell,
The kernel *is* there, sound and sweet,
Sweeter than luscious fruit which fell
O'er-ripe and ready at your feet.

As diamond keen, as diamond true !
Trust her with aught, *she'll* never tell.
My secrets !   Yes, she knows a few,
Don't you, my old companion, Nell ?

N.

Friend of my heart, with the eyes so true
That they grappled my love in a glance to you,
And such a dimple in either cheek,
Where Cupid nestles in hide-and-seek—
Soft and sweet are the thoughts which rise
To the charm of your answering sympathies

Only a murmuring echo yet !
Only a faint, far-off sound to tell
Of ocean's whisper above the shell
Where the soul lies sleeping, the pearl is set.
An unused harp, with the rusting wires
Half quivering only with vague desires,
Unconscious thrills of a music, dumb
In silent sleep, till its time shall come.
But let Love's passionate fingers ring
With firm, strong hand, o'er each waken'd string,
Or sorrow touch them, or suffering,
Such grand, sweet music would wake and start
From quicken'd soul and unfolded heart ;
Such earnest purpose and steadfast will,
And woman's power to do and bear,
That startled listeners, hush'd and still,
Would cry, " 'Twas a heroine unaware."

I think that there comes to us once in our lives,
Perhaps once only, however sought,
Just *that*, for which each in dim longing strives,
The grand key-note of our souls and thought.

To some it is sounded in early youth,
For a life-long anthem of work and truth ;
To others it comes 'neath the midday sun,
And a glorious battle is fought and won ;
To others, alas ! it is only given
With their feet on the borderland of Heaven.

May God send it, friend of my heart, to thee,
When the will and the wish and the fate agree !

Ξ.

A guardian angel of the house !
With no pretence of angel wings,
Or shining halo round her brows ;
Too glorious for common things.

But, like the briony which creeps
Where parch'd highways with dust are white,
Or, like the glowworm lamp which peeps
Through all the gathering gloom of night,

The clash and ring of glorious deeds
May pass her with their stirring cry,
But little, pressing, daily needs
Grow lighter as she passes by.

For where life's path is over-thick
With tangled briars which catch and fray,
Her hand, regardless scratch or prick,
Will gently clear the thorns away.

Or where the jarring discords ring,
When Love's best notes are out of tune,
Her hand will from the loosen'd string
Coax melody like birds in June.

And if grim Trouble's icy clutch,
Or pain's hot, scathing tear-drops fall,
Her quiet voice and gentle touch
Are simply perfect—that is all !

O.

Stand forth, my friend ! with soft hair smoothly
  banded
Across your matron brow sedate and fair ;
A brow which falsehood never yet has branded,
Nor envy traced his crooked footsteps there.

White, dimpled hands, whereon the diamonds glitter
Like lilies sprinkled with fresh drops of dew,
So soft and careless as they flash and flitter,
In friendship's grasp so loyal and so true.

And clear, blue eyes like pools of limpid beauty,
Where Love's forget-me-nots are hush'd asleep,
Whilst sweet serenity and earnest duty,
Like two shy water-fays behind them peep ;

Yet in their depths the netted sunlight flashes,
As mirth's gay fireflies on the ripples dance,
And underneath the golden, curling lashes,
Darts many a bright look or a saucy glance.

Fair be your life, with little trace of sadness !
Care's weary sighs be stifled in their birth !
For purer nature never thrill'd to gladness ;
No kinder heart is beating on God's earth.

II.

Stroke a poll, Poll !   Nay ! now who could resist it ?
Seeing that pate with its smooth golden hair,
Just as if Sol in a transport had kissed it,
And left some sunbeams behind, unaware.

Sit for your portrait at once, and don't fidget !
Can't you keep quiet, you wee, restless thing ?
Just for the world like a troublesome midget,
Fond of the sunshine and quick with its sting.

That is *the sketch*, but the details are missing !
Not *there* the portrait of somebody ends.
Dearest of lips ever fashion'd for kissing,
Sweetest of nurses and truest of friends.
Ah ! when my girdle of jewels I measure,
Silently giving to each one her due,
Pausing awhile o'er the ones I most treasure,
Bright 'mid the brightest I find little Loo.

P.

Amid chrysanthemums' soft blaze of splendour,
Amid the gentle memories autumn brings,
Among sweet thoughts—the sweetest and most
    tender
Which Time from out the Past's low echo rings,
You come surrounded by unfading spell,
Fair as the name they gave you—Isabel !

With hopes and fears that long ago have blended
In bless'd reality of love and trust ;
With brightest dreams that in fruition ended
Without one vision crumbling into dust ;
With happiness that like God's sunshine fell,
I link your matron beauty—Isabel !

Σ.

Bright-eyed, keen-witted, with a glance as keen !
A woman who has brought her woman's tact
To teach her sister-women how to *act*,
And give dull lives the diamond's glittering sheen.

Who, what her hand hath found at hand to do,
Has done with active brain and earnest might,
And, like the starlight shining through the night,
Has watch'd and waited till the morning grew.

What if the dawning seem delay'd, my friend,
Work on in faith ! the darkest hours are past,
The day-star rises, and there comes at last
The glorious sunlight without break or end !

T.

When all dread Sorrow's rosary of pain
Is counted out, each bead let slowly fall,
Like suffering's tears in heavy drops of rain,
We say of you, " She has endured them all ! "

One priceless gift Time's hand in mercy deals,
The hope that underneath all trouble lies :
You fall between the Juggernaut's dread wheels,
And look beyond to blue and cloudless skies.

And so at last—God grant it may be soon—
The wailing dirge of sorrow must be hush'd ;
And this world hold some bright, unchequer'd boon,
For that brave spirit—stunn'd, but never crush'd.

T.
In Memoriam.

Dark eyes that gleam'd from out thy shadowy hair,
With strange, sad beauty that was half divine ;
And sweet, low, ringing voice whose pathos rare,
Caught every heart as by a silken snare,
    And made all thine !

How wondrous was the melody which stole
Beneath thy fingers, when the ivory keys
Thrill'd to thy touch, and pour'd their hidden soul
In music such as genius can control
        With perfect ease.

Ah ! child ! those eyes have their full beauty now.
That soft, low voice thrills to the angels' song ;
The asphodel—not laurel—wreathes thy brow,
And glory, more than earth's poor gifts allow,
        Was thine ere long !

We cannot wish thee back !   Our tearful eyes
With pity for our loss alone are wet.
Thine is the gain ! through faith our sorrows rise,
And, knowing thou art safe in Paradise,
        Love stills regret !

Φ.

Friend of these later days ! whose locks loose-braided
Are such as artists love to watch and paint,
When 'mid dim tints and glories softly shaded
They draw their dream of martyr or of saint ;

And clear, calm eyes, lit with the light of reason,
The quicken'd insight into means and ways,
Which show the common sense that's most in season
In these high-pressure, nineteenth-century days.

Ay, but I love you best when, softly dreaming,
You soar beyond the world of commonplace,
And, half unconsciously your white arms' gleaming
Adds to the starlight beauty of your face—
And yet, my dear, the world of dreamy beauty
Lies far beyond our mortal sight and ken ;
The practical, stern path of daily duty
Fits us the best to serve our fellow-men.

And you *are* practical ! e'en poets tire
Of soaring always to the heights sublime,
Nature is human, and an o'erstretch'd wire
Cracks into uselessness before its time.
We want the highest ever set before us !
Let the divinest voices have full sway,
But common sense must swell the after-chorus—
And so, my dear, I love you either way !

X.

Hey ! my old colleagues ! 'mid the roll of friends
Whose names I write in letters of pure gold,
A thousand kindly thoughts my memory sends
Towards each of you, as each one's name is told :
And the quick stir of mutual interest lends
A heighten'd charm to those glad days of old.

Nor do I count it triumph mean or small
That, 'mid the rush of varying views and ways,
Not one short word of anger was let fall
In any dealings of those busy days.
With pride I say that I am " friends with all,"
With pride you hear it—yours the due and praise !

Not one forgetting, and by none forgot !
'Tis sweet to say so, after three years' test,
Then take, for each of you a tiny knot
Of pansies—"that's for thoughts"—my warmest, best :
A bright-eyed tuft of blue forget-me-not,
And bays to crown you, when work yields to rest !

l.

Ψ.

Little daughter, with grey-blue eyes
Lit by a million coquetries !
Little daughter, whose restless will
Like aspen's flutter is never still !
Little daughter, whose every sense
Breathes the perfume of innocence !

Little you reck that the world grows old,
Evil, dreary, crafty, and cold ;
That time flies sweeping his hard, grey wings
O'er the bloom of the fairest things,
And the love and beauty the angels lay
Round your childish footsteps must fade away !

There's no resting for you, my sweet,
Life's path waits for those eager feet ;
Every step as you journey on,
Some hope lost, or some pure faith gone ;
Until the smouldering embers throw
But a flickering shadow of youth's bright glow.

*　　*　　*　　*　　*

Yet, my darling, I scarcely pray
For your footsteps too smooth a way !
Rather I'd crown you with myrrh and rue
Than sunniest roses wet with dew ;
For every sorrow *your* heart must know,
A myriad graces will burst and blow ;

Every thorn in your weary feet
Will make the pathway of others sweet ;
Every drop that your wrung heart bleeds,
A drop of pity for her who needs.
'Tis only by suffering keenly, we
Learn the crown of womanhood—sympathy.

Ω.

There ! I have painted them, old and young.
   Those whom my pen like a row of pearls
On the golden thread of my love has strung,
   A snowy girdle of women and girls—
Never a ruby amongst the row—
Men have no place in my heart, you know !

Yet for the sake of those hazel eyes,
   Where my life, like a new Narcissus, bending
In its own reflection, faints and dies
   In wedded love that can know no ending,
I'll own there is sometimes—*just now and then*—
A friend, worthy friendship, amongst the men.

For half reproachful those eyes of brown
   Glance sharply up from the nuts and wine,
And eyes of blue look so softly down
   They challenge a gentle look from mine!
And ah! nay, I could not turn away
From the kindly warmth of those eyes of grey.

And many a memory true and tried
   With a glimpse of a brown moustache appear'd,
And thoughts of genuine liking hide
   Within the folds of a tawny beard—
Nay, I must stop!—or, in truth, my pen
Will find too many amongst the men.

A HANDFUL OF VERSES.

A HANDFUL OF VERSES.

A GREETING.

" ALL hail ! " the New Year cries
With the first grey dawn of light.
In yonder sky see the red sun rise
O'er the mountain's frosted white.
    And thus I come to you !
Let your strong young hopes arise,
And fight their way with fresh strength anew
Through the mists of cloudy skies.
    Sorrow I needs must bring,
For on earth no soul hath rest ;
But it may be, too, that your heart shall sing
With the hopes of a lifetime bless'd.

THREE SHOTS.

STOOD a dainty little maid,
Blue eyes, dreamy, hazy;
Dimpled face, where blushes laid
Like a pink-tipp'd daisy.
Came a smooth-chinn'd boy close by.
Cupid watch'd all ready,
Shot them both through hand and eye.
Eh! 'twas aim unsteady.

Stood a maiden fair to see,
Charms had she in plenty,
Crown'd by maiden dignity
At staid two-and-twenty.
Came a man hot, eager, young,
For life's battle ready.
Cupid shot through lip and tongue.
Eh! 'twas aim unsteady.

Stood a woman in her prime,
Youth's first pinions folded,
All the wavering gifts of time
Thirty years had moulded.

Came a man whose shoulders square
Challenged any comers,
Whose firm eyes and grizzling hair
Told of forty summers.

Cupid watch'd them both awhile,
Fingering his arrows.
" Toys," he mutter'd, with a smile,
" For my mother's sparrows."
Then he chose one piercing dart,
And in godlike fashion
Shot them both straight through the heart.
That's the age for passion !

QUAKER COUSINS.

MAY, fresh, leafy May is here !
Month of poets, garlands, greetings,
Cutting east wind, sunshine clear,
    And May meetings.

Turning down by Bishopsgate,
Where are all the quiet dresses
Marking, by their folds sedate,
    Quakeresses ?

'Neath the scuttle bonnet's rim
Each face every inch a lady ;
Where's the hat with ample brim,
    Broad and shady ?

Where the gentle " thee " and " thou,"
Soft as ring-dove's low caresses ?
Ah ! they're gone and vanish'd now,
    Quakeresses !

And I grieve, as one *can* grieve
Over other people's trippings,
That of such sweet ways you leave
    Scarce the clippings.

If *my* feet should ever stray
To the faith of my forefathers,
I'll insist on dresses grey,
    All round gathers,

Pure white kerchief, spotless shawl,
Snowy cap—depend upon it,
And, my cousins, more than all,
    That poke bonnet.

For a face its charm beneath
Blossoms into soften'd beauty,
Like a lily in its sheath
    Held by duty.

Once in that old, narrow street
Lovely faces smiled by dozens,
Once each step or two I'd meet
    Quaker cousins.

And though I was in the lurch,
All of Quaker blood inherit,
Whatso'er their creed or church,
    Quaker spirit.

Two gifts they will ever hold,
Theirs in every clime and nation,
Art of coining honest gold
    And—flirtation !

Of the former I despair,
But perhaps it doesn't matter,
Fate gave me a double share
    Of the latter.

LINES ON A PORTRAIT.

THERE are women for whom men will struggle and
　　lie,
Will hold faith and honour and peace less dear ;
Ay, women for whom they will live or die ;
　　　But you are not one, my dear !

There are women whose voices ring through all time
Fearless and true, as a clarion clear,
Others with lives like the sweet church-bells' chime ;
　　　You're neither of those, my dear !

There are women who love till their hearts' full beat
Throbs, ay, to breaking, for *one* to hear,
Whose life love has forged to a still, white heat ;
　　　You're not one of those, my dear !

There are women who meekly tread day by day
A slow round of duty in faith and fear,
Who patiently dribble their lives away ;
　　　You're not one of those, my dear !

Your face is as fair as a face may be,
But there isn't one troubling angel near
To stir up its pretty monotony ;
    You'll never miss *that*, my dear !

Life's strongest wine leaves a headache behind,
Safer, more wholesome, is watery small beer ;
In that dead level *my* feet never find,
    You will be happy, my dear !

You'll amble by in the world's eager race,
Pack'd in a nutshell your travelling gear ;
Children, and servants, and jewels, and lace,
    And—nothing farther, my dear !

POPULAR.

I WROTE some verses, and I thought
Them rather stupid, but I knew
The market where such things are bought,
And so I sold them. Would not you ?
And with the guinea in my purse,
I felt I'd solved an honest claim ;
I that much better—none the worse.
Fair business, but, of course, not Fame.

Then by-and-bye the people said—
You know the silly sort of way—
It was the " prettiest " thing they'd read
For this, and that, and many a day !
Pleased ?   Well, perhaps, and yet not quite,
Because I thought the thing so tame,
I wish'd I'd kept it out of sight,
Nor hazarded my hope of Fame.

'Twas copied here, 'twas copied there !
At every turn it met my eyes,
Until I sigh'd, in sheer despair,
" I really thought the world more wise."
We like applause, we folks who sing !
The people's praise, the critics' blame,
But then, we like it for a thing
That gives us just a chance of Fame.

One day,—'twas at a country inn,
A crippled child of nine or ten,
With pallid features, pinch'd and thin,
Watch'd every movement of my pen.

"Mrs. Frank Snoad?" I bent my head ;
"Yes, little one ; that is my name."
"I know your 'Curly Locks,'" she said.
It sounded like a glimpse of Fame.

Next in the Winchester express,
A fellow-traveller, on a box
Beside me read out my address,
And smiled, "Then you wrote 'Curly Locks'!"
Ah ! lordly poets, wear your crown,
I'll envy not your bigger game,
My baby-daughter snatch'd me down
At any rate a *glimpse* of Fame.

FIRST AND LAST.

UNDERNEATH the lilac's
Heart-leaves bending down,
Fragrant perfume wafted
From their blossom-crown ;
By the reeds and rushes,
Oh ! if eyes had seen !
Kiss'd ? Ah ! spare the blushes
Of new-fledged sixteen.

Sweet is Love's first dawning,
When his wings unfold,
Not one soft grey warning
In the pinions gold ;
Sweet the swallow's flying
O'er a world of bliss ;
Sweet the pleasure lying
In a stolen kiss.

Ah ! that trembling rapture,
Such as cannot last !
Who could Love recapture
When his flight is past ?
Memory clothes the vision
With a tender glow,
For those fields Elysian
Are—so long ago.

Then, as lightly skimming
O'er the roll of years,
Life's cup's fill'd to brimming,
Half with joy, half tears ;

Lovers, lovers, lovers,
Thick as leaves are cast ;
Memory only hovers
O'er the first and last.

Sweet has been the wooing,
Of full many a tongue,
Sweet Love's glad pursuing,
Whilst the world was young.
From my heart I pity
Maidens loved by one ;
Dozens storm'd the city,
Ere my life was won.

But, beneath the lilacs,
When the sunlight stole
Through the rainy evening,
Love knock'd at my soul :
Though 'twas long years after,
When he caught me fast.
Others are but details,
There's *one* first, *one* last.

WELL MATCHED.

A YOUTH stood watching a maiden's eyes as he
would watch for ever,
He thought himself most worldly-wise, far-seeing,
'cute, and clever ;
Two powers warr'd in angry strife as he stood
hesitating,
And Love and Prudence both were rife, in argument
debating.

Love whisper'd, " She is all to you ; go, make her
even nearer !"
Said Prudence, " Pause ere you pursue, remember
gold is dearer."
Cried Love, " For shame ! go win your way in honest,
manly fashion."
Quoth Prudence, " Who but fools obey the promptings
of such passion ?"

Said Love, " Your arguments are cold — nay, worse
than cold, they're cruel ;
Why ! count her love as wealth untold, her trust a
priceless jewel."

Said Prudence, " Ay, but does she bring position as
    a dower?
Real, solid influence is the thing to back up beauty's
    power."

Said Love, "Your heart is beating fast for her, and
    for her only ;
Though all the world were yours at last, without her
    you'd be lonely."
Quoth Prudence, " Love soon fades, methinks, if
    Fortune's thorns are prickly,
 The rattle of the golden chinks will cure your heart-
    ache quickly."

Cried Love, " Not so ! my power is deep, and often
    shall I chide you ;
Lull memory, if you can, to sleep ; indifference beside
    you ?
No ; dare the worst for love and truth ! that blush
    tells you can get her."
Cried Prudence, " Hold !" and sway'd the youth in
    spirit and in letter.

     .   .   .   .   .   .

Weeks came and went, as I have heard, the youth to
    love still willing,
When one day sang a little bird news setting each
    pulse thrilling :
" Young man, you've made a slight mistake ! your
    prudence has misled you !
There's wealth and influence at stake ; be off ! and
    make her wed you."

Off sped the youth at railway pace, no second sum-
    mons needing ;
Though smiles lit up the maiden's face, she tried to
    seem unheeding ;
He pleaded long and tenderly, all thoughts of lucre
    scorning,
But wise as well as fair was she ; her answer was,
    " Good morning."

A STORY OF LONG AGO.

The enemy's forces are strong without,
And the castle's warriors, brave and stout,
Shake their grizzled heads in foreboding doubt.

They have fought their best to o'erwhelming
    odds,
They have fought like warriors, ay, like gods !
But the siege is long and they're sorely tried ;
Yet they'll victors be, if they can but wait,
For help is theirs, so the force outside
Make not the succour a day too late.

A murmur rises amid them all :
Is there knight or dame who hath aught to say ?
Is there one amongst us, great or small,
Who hath a counsel to give to-day ?

Spake the aged crone with the wrinkled brow :
" Ye need never have cause to fear !
Hold fast by the ancient formula and no foe can
    enter here !
You have but to tie up the western gate, when the
    evening sun goes down,
With the threefold cord as your fathers did, and
    which oft hath saved the town :
One strand of rope that is newly-spun 'twixt the
    morn and evening light,

One strand of chain that is freshly forged, with its
　　shining links still bright,
And one of hair from a maiden's head, whose fame is
　　of spotless white."

You can hear the forge's hammers beat as the red
　　sparks gleam and fly ;
Through the morning cool and the noonday heat, the
　　weaver's shuttles ply ;
A maiden kneels at her lady's feet, with a prayer
　　pray'd earnestly.
" Lady, my sires have fought for yours in the days
　　that are past and gone ;
My sire left *me* to win the spurs, since brothers I have
　　none,
And I claim my right for your cause to fight, as a
　　maiden may alone—

I swear by the holy Bread and Wine, by the awful
　　mystic Three,
There was never a thought or act of mine which is
　　not purity !"

There is not a voice in the castle there can whisper
    aught of shame,
But old and young in one breath declare of white,
    unsullied fame—
Chaste as the violet in the wood, cold as the falling
    snow,
Pure as snowdrop's opening bud, or the mountain
    torrent's flow.

They have craved a truce till the sun goes down,
Till the spell is ready to save the town,
The chain and rope are a goodly pair,
They need but the maiden's golden hair.

Clothed in garments of virgin white,
As a bride might be for the marriage rite,
They lead her forth, and the look she wears
Is worthy the noble name she bears—
A look of triumph, as if to say
" I rank with your bravest knights to-day ! "
Meekly she kneels at the altar there,
And her lips just part in unspoken prayer ;

Then the white-robed priest, with the lily hand,
Utters a blessing smooth and bland.
And hymns are chanted and prayers are pray'd,
Whilst the scissors play round her shapely
    head ;
The golden locks on the shrine are laid,
And the last brief blessing devoutly said.

Forth through the castle-yard she goes,
With her close-cropp'd waves of glistening hair,
A sight to charm either friends or foes.
And the men's loud plaudits ring on the air,
For the weakest heart in the coming fight
Feels that the battle is theirs to-night !

Swiftly the death-dealing arrows fly
From cunning holes which no foe can spy ;
Hotly, thickly the arrows fall
From the foes without—over tower and wall ;
Fiercer, fiercer the contest rages,
When night is o'er, and the day dawns fast ;
But the castle force still the battle wages,
For victory must be theirs at last !

Then a cry of horror!   The gates are down !
The enemy's forces throng the town !
Death !   Who was false ?   Not that giant chain !
Not the hempen rope !—they have done their best.
'Twas the golden hair could not bear the strain ;
Those lying locks that the good priest bless'd,
No maid's were they !   Ay, the truth's confess'd !

But the foremost knight, with the snowy crest,
Has dash'd that furious band aside,
Has caught his *wife* to his sheltering breast
And " No maid !—matron ! " proudly cried.
Deep go the spurs in his charger's side,
Though they strive to tear her limb from limb ;
He has clear'd the town ! and the gates yawn wide,
He has saved the life of his love and bride—
False to her kindred but true to him !

ESCULAPIUS.

A LOT of puppets with wires all wrong,
Limbs twisted round, and their joints awry,
But I shall set them to rights ere long.
A workman fond of his work am I !

I've plenty of patience and plenty of brain ;
My puppets will most of them dance again.

Here's this old chap with a broken shin,
A glorious task for a mender's skill,
Just see the tacks I am driving in,
The glue I heat with a right good will ;
Then here's another with broken springs,
He'll dance if they're careful about the strings !

Another doll with a pretty face,
Her joints all faulty, some broken quite ;
Here, twist this round to its proper place,
And peg the others !—there ! she's all right.
The trouble is nothing at all to me ;
I'm mending my puppet fast, you see.

This one ! a nasty crack in the head,
His springs all gone, and a broken limb ;
He has to dance for his daily bread,
I can't help feeling sorry for him.
What folly !—I can but do my best
For him—as I do for all the rest.

I grudge no trouble, no pains I spare,
I love my work and I like to see
These broken toys in the world's great Fair
Dance all the merrier, thanks to me :
" As good as ever," the people say,
A clever workman has pass'd our way.

One puppet heard—she was only wood,
Her fibres merely of temper'd steel,
No living woman of flesh and blood,
But puppets sometimes can think and feel—
And she thought, "He is mending them all, I
    see,
But the best may fail when they come to me."

She had play'd the part of a mimic queen,
And said to herself, with a bitter sigh :
" My part is over, they've changed the scene,
And dropp'd the curtain—'tis best to die.
Ah ! workman, in pity cut the string ;
Why try to tinker a worthless thing ? "

MY IDEAL.

No hero form'd of wisdom and of power,
Endow'd with virtues boundless and untold ;
But one whose love can sweeten every hour,
And turn the clods of common earth to gold.

No visionary sage whose will unerring
Can guide mine own in rapturous trust intense ;
But one, by turns deferr'd to and deferring,
Who simply follows honest common sense.

No dreamer vow'd to theory and beauty,
With aims so glorious, none their heights may
      ken;
But one who faithfully just does his duty,
And fears no man amongst his fellow-men.

No lordly leader I must follow after,
In meek devotion pampering every whim ;
But one who, hand in hand, come tears, come
      laughter,
Is all to me, as I am all to him.

*   *   *   *   *   *

Ideal, did I say ?   Nay, that's all over !
My dream has stood rough wedlock's sternest test,
And since my husband took the place of lover,
" Ideal " is a portrait at the best.

CURLY LOCKS.

CURLY locks, curly locks, what angel brought you
Down to this world in your mischievous glee ?
Curly locks, curly locks, what angel thought you
Just the right gift for your father and me ?
Nobody wanted you ; no one invited you ;
You were quite welcome to stay up above ;
Yet you arrived, and then who could have slighted you?
Bringing as luggage a bundle of love.

Curly locks, curly locks, tell me who taught you
That wicked glance of your roguish blue eyes ?
Are you *quite* sure 'twas an angel who brought you,
You imp of mischief in baby disguise ?
Why did the angels with kisses half smother
You, who now reign as my nursery queen ?
See, here's a dimple, and here is another !
Each dimple shows where a kiss must have been.

Curly locks, curly locks, made up of laughter,
Merriment, nonsense, caresses, and fun,
Just a few tears that the smiles follow after,
Quickly as dew-drops are chased by the sun
Knowing yet nothing of sorrow and sadness,
Guessing at nothing of envy and strife ;
Long may it be ere Time, stifling your gladness,
Brushes the bloom from your innocent life.

THE SURGEON'S BAG.

A BAG that can make the pluckiest pale,
When the yawning mouth tells its ghastly tale,
And those silent instruments gleaming lie,
'Neath whose touch all suffer and many die ;
The stoutest hero's proved nerves might flag
At very thought of the surgeon's bag.

See the white, scared faces around the bed,
Where, like a pall, hangs the hush of dread ;
Whilst the friends talk on, and the patient hears
With that forced confidence born of fears,
And the busy tongues of the neighbours wag,
" That's the surgeon come !   Did you see his bag ?"

The window's open to let the fume
Of chloroform's blessing from out the room ;
He takes his fee, and he drives away.
" One more life given a chance to-day ! "
Thank God ! train'd skill, not mere empty brag,
Is the guiding force of the surgeon's bag.

CHIPPENDALE CHAIRS.

A HUSBAND and wife were holding a cabinet council
    of two,
For the subject on hand was weighty, one of life's
    practical cares ;
And a bright little pitcher sat listening, as bright
    little pitchers will do,
To every detail of " moving,"—new curtains and carpets
    and chairs.

" But, mother ! " she broke in at last (for 'twas getting
    quite *too* much to bear),
Her cheeks dimpled deep with excitement, like rose-
    petals curved into bloom,

" There'll be new things for nurse and for father, the
　　drawing-room—*everywhere !*
What is there coming from London to put in your own
　　little room ? "

The mother look'd laughingly down, with a sparkle of
　　fun in her eyes,
" Why, money is getting so scarce, there'll be none left
　　to spend upon me,
I must have your old, nursery things!"　Then the sor-
　　rowful look of surprise,
And the horrified droop of the lips was a comical
　　picture to see.

A week, perhaps more, had gone by, when the little
　　maid came all aglow,
So good and so happy that morning, as lightly she
　　tripp'd down the stairs :
" See, mother, I've brought you my penny, 'tis for your
　　little room ; don't you know
You said that you couldn't afford it ?　Won't this help
　　to buy Chippendale chairs ? "

　　　*　　　　*　　　　*　　　　*　　　　*

Ah ! little one, hold fast the secret ! to turn life's dull
    pence into gold,
To find how much sweetness and solace from self's
    bitter herbs can be press'd ;
Let that sunshine of thinking for others love's blossoms
    of beauty unfold,
And your life will grow glad in their fragrance, for they
    who give blessing are bless'd.

WALLFLOWERS.

THEY were boy and girl together
In the length'ning days of spring,
Fickle moods of changeful weather
When the nestlings take to wing.
In that quaint old cottage-garden
Who could dream of after-pain
Sweet offence, and sweeter pardon,
'Mid the wallflowers wet with rain ?

Too swiftly came a parting,
Soon the halcyon days were o'er ;
And a girl's full heart was smarting
O'er the lad she saw no more.

N

ECHOES OF LIFE.

Not a word of love was spoken,
For they knew that hope was vain ;
But he gave her as a token
Some wallflowers wet with rain.

All the flash of war's red glory
She has read with bated breath,
Has grown glorious o'er his glory,
Though it sow'd the seeds of death.
Still she lives, not sad nor lonely,
For the solace of all years
Is the gift he sent her—only
Some wallflowers wet with tears.

A SONG OF SUMMER.

Down by the wide old gate we stood,
Which creak'd upon its rusty hinges,
The broad nut walk, that hedged the wood
   With russet fringes,
Hid us from every passer-by.
No fear of those thick leaves betraying,
They only heard with sympathy
   What we were saying.

For youth was young, and love was new,
And very fast our hearts were beating ;
We linger'd on, and hardly knew
    How time was fleeting.
Then—" Would that we had never met ! "
For love was strong and pride was stronger—
We parted, trying to forget
    And love no longer.

Again in summer-time we stood
Both bending o'er a bunch of roses.
Ay, every look (it was no good)
    The truth discloses.
And if my heart had beaten fast,
That summer day it beat much faster ;
Love conquer'd pride, and, tamed at last,
    It own'd love master !

Now years have flown, through sun and rain
We've sung and braved all sorts of weather ;
No trouble crushing heart or brain
    If borne together.

We've had our share of smiles and tears,
And, through all changes grim or pleasant,
We never loved in all those years
    As in the present.

Old folks not love, and love die out !
Be quiet, silly lads and lasses,
You know not what you talk about ;
    For as Time passes
He pulls the clover by the ears,
Laughs at the cherries freshly fruited ;
But knows that for a hundred years
    The holly's rooted.

PUCK.

Somewhere or other the fairies still lurk,
Spite of the prose of this practical world,
Spite of the turmoil of hurry and work,
Deep in the blossoms and buds they lie curl'd.
Who cares for salt that he helps not himself ?
Who does not thrill at a horse-shoe for "luck" ?
There ! lay your wisdom aside on a shelf !
Else you can never be friendly with Puck.

Many a time Puck has flown off to me ;
All the gold blossom-dust thick on his wings,
Brightest of bright, sunny Elfland is he,
Careless and gay as the songs that he sings.
Childhood, perhaps, was his favourite time ;
For, when Love's gong beat the summons to life,
Puck stood aghast at the sonorous chime,
Liking a maiden much better than wife.

Then came the war-cry " To arms ! " and it rang
Right through my soul with an echo that stirr'd
Every pulse with its thundering clang ;
Ay, and I answered ! " To arms ! " at a word.
Ay, and I fought ! with heart, lips, thought, and pen—
Fought, until fainting I sank by the way.
Puck was most terribly scared at me then,
Spread forth his wings and flew frighten'd away.

But Puck is faithful ! when weariness came,
Useless the days and the hours so long,
I'd but to smile and to call him by name,
Hither he flew with his gambols and song,

Perch'd on the sunbeams, in wild, elfish glee,
Gather'd the motes for his playthings all day,
Call'd to the sparrows, and coax'd in a bee,
That I might see how he rode it away.

Told me such tales, as at evening he peer'd
Into the fire and read stories there ;
Made up such legends, some graceful, some weird,
Laugh'd at depression and fought off despair ;
Knew all the flowers' love-stories, and told
Just what the spiders and flies were about ;
Harness'd the fancies I loved so of old,
Lest I should fear all my dreams were play'd out.

Puck has one failing, I needs must confess !
Being a fairy, he recks nought of time ;
Just as a sunbeam he'll kiss and caress,
Then the next moment make merry with rime ;
So he cares nothing for day or for night,
And in the night, *how* he drives sleep away !
Puck, precious Puck ; wee elf, winsome and bright ;
I'm only mortal, *do* come here by day !

A SILENT SERMON.

Cover'd up warmly the strawberries lie,
The rose-tree stems are barren and bare,
The faded leaves on the poplar die,
There's sleepy quietude everywhere!
But they shout to me, "Oh! mistress mine,
Why didn't you learn the lesson we teach—
Lesson as clear as a printed line :
Work and rest must each come to each.

" *We* wait calmly under the snow,
Sure that the spring will in time come round,
Glad to be restful and quiet ; we know
Thus the bright summer with beauty is crown'd.
You must needs crave for a summer all year,
You must needs blossom in spite of the frost,
Bud out of season—but ah! mistress dear,
What did you gain beside that you have lost ?

" Take home the lesson ! a long winter now !
All the months miss'd of the fog and the rain
You must endure, to Nature must bow
Until your spring-time shall come round again.

Rest, mistress, rest, like your flowers be still,
Practise our preaching and quietly lie ;
Some day glad sunshine the whole world will fill,
Some day the swallows will skim 'cross the sky."

Ah ! ye who read, hear the voice of the flowers,
List to the sermon that's preach'd by the trees,
Mingle with work all the soft dreamy hours,
When life sinks down on a cushion of ease.
" Lazy ?" *I* thought so.   " Too quiet ?" Ah! yes,
I have said that in the days that are past,
But there's one truth that in strength we don't guess,
Over-work means but a break-down at last.

THIRTY.

THE glow of the dawn is gone and past,
The sun is up and 'tis full midday,
Time's shadow athwart my path is cast,
And youth has kiss'd me and flown away.
Hey for the past where the dewdrops clung
Fresh with their tremulous hopes and fears !
Hey for the time when the world was young,
Nor dreaded the climax of thirty years !

Twenty is over!   My footsteps pass
On to a decade, whose cold east wind
Blows every blossom from bough and grass,
Leaving fast ripening fruit behind.
Never a beauty or charm remains,
But Age with his withering touch soon scars.
After summer come autumn rains,
'Tis all down hill after thirty years!

And I see, for mirrors *they* tell the truth,
Already some tresses are fleck'd with grey,
Life follow'd Time like a weeping Ruth,
When this morning's dawn banish'd yesterday.
The reign of folly is over now,
And in place of joy's garland of oats appears
A prudent matron with sober brow,
One *must* grow sober at thirty years!

Ay, girls and boys, 'tis your time for play—
Mine's over now, I must step aside,
Yet I own that the other side the way
Looks bleak and chilly this bright springtide.

May I borrow a year or two from you?
"Nay," wisdom whispers, "Time's cruel shears
Deal best with those who to Time are true,"
So here's content to my thirty years!

1884.

Part II.

CLARE PEYCE'S DIARY.

AS LIFE ITSELF.

MY DIARY.

April 3rd.

THERE isn't *one* thing that has gone right to-day !
   And now they've refused the De Guestenet's ball !
It's downright provoking !   I'm in such a way,
   And long for that pet of a Harold to call.
The waltzes I'd promised and saved up for him !
   I felt quite convinced that at last he'd propose ;
And now it's all done for, through some foolish whim,
   And how I am fidgeting nobody knows !

To-morrow, it seems, we are going to dine
   With some one or other (they're strangers to me),
To meet the Mark Smythes and a cousin of mine,
   My rich banker cousin, the Chesney M.P.

It's years since we've seen him ; in fact, I can't say
   If I've ever seen him, 'tis so long ago ;
I seem to remember he call'd here one day
   When I was a child, and he thirty or so.

   April 4th.

I just snatch a moment to sit down and write,
   That Harold has call'd, as I hoped for, to-day ;
We weren't left alone, but he squeezed my hand *tight*,
   As much as to hint he had something to say.
Young Hamilton pass'd, too, and gave such a
     bow—
   He isn't quite heart-whole I know very well.
Dear me ! it is six !   I must go and dress now,
   And show my dear cousin the Sevenoaks belle.

   April 4th.
     „   *5th.*

We had such a glorious evening last night,
   I did so enjoy it ! yet hardly know why :
There were only our hostess, her sister Miss White,
   The Mark Smythes, my cousin, my parents, and I.

My cousin is forty if he is a day,
  As handsome a man, though, as you'd wish to see ;
He talked to mamma most, yet still, in his way,
  I thought he was rather attentive to me.

He's five or six children, it seems, of his own ;
  He's now been a widower nearly four years ;
He spoke of his loss—and his living alone,
  And the tone of his voice almost moved me to tears.
What rubbish it is to write thus ! but it's true ;
  His children no doubt are all left to run wild ;
He's ask'd me to stay with them—so I will too,
  But surely he doesn't think me a mere child !

I talk'd well last night, not mere rubbish and stuff,
  As I might had my cousin been likely to flirt,
But sensible talk, staid and proper enough
  For the highest-dried bore, whoe'er button'd a shirt,
I went in for politics, literature, art,
  Ah ! and science as well, as I can if I choose ;
It was playing, I know, a most venturesome part,
  But I fancy he rather admires the " blues."

At any rate now he can't think me a fool,
  Though twice in the evening that horrid Miss
    White
Ask'd me if I was out ? and if I had left school ?
  I'm sure it was nothing but envy and spite.
She's trying to catch Cousin Clifton, I know,
  As if he would have her—a vicious old maid !
She's thirty, satirical, " blue,"—oh ! no ! no !
  He'll never care for her—*I* am not afraid.

April 6th.
  „ *7th.*
  „ *8th.*

    My cousin Clifton call'd to-day,
      He's very handsome, if not young,
    He's ask'd me there again to stay—
      Why did I blush and hold my tongue ?
    Am I ?—good gracious, it's absurd—
      The fact is I was rather shy,
    That must be it—upon my word
      I don't know what it is—not I—

But Cousin Clifton seems to be
    So different from other men,
A sort of demigod to me,
    I have such fancies now and then.
And he's so clever and so wise,
    So worshipp'd by all sorts of sets,
I'd like to stand well in his eyes,
    Though Harold *is* my pet of pets.

April 9*th*.
   ,,   10*th*.

I went out for a stroll to-day,
    Because my cousin still is here,
But Miss White drove the other way
    And he was with her—that's *quite* clear.

Oh! Harold call'd while I was out,
    And really I am rather glad,
He's fond of me, I have no doubt,
    But I can't marry such a lad.

He's very, very nice, but then
    He's barely three and twenty yet;
I don't like juvenile young men—
    They're all such youngsters in our set.

April 11th.

„   *12th.*

„   *13th.*

My cousin call'd to say good-bye,
    And hoped, when next I wanted change,
That I should be induced to try
    The Surrey air at Morecomb Grange.

And then, before he went away,
    My guardian angel made him speak
The words I long'd for—" Fix the day "—
    And so I fix'd it for next week.

Our talk was merely simple chat—
    Knole Park, the neighbourhood, the ball,
The Smythe's pug dog, and things like that—
    One thing, though, made me rather small.

He seem'd so anxious I should go,
    I thought " Perhaps he'll squeeze my hand."
I look'd down when I gave it—*no*,
    That style he doesn't understand.

Still colouring, I raised my eyes,
    And he look'd back at me again,
So quietly—half in surprise—
    He must have thought me very vain.

He isn't smitten—no, not he !—
    No more than is yon kingly sun
Enamour'd of that droning bee—
    He beams alike on every one.

April 14*th.*
    „   15*th.*
    „   16*th.*
    „   17*th.*
    „   18*th.*
    „   19*th.*
    „   20*th.*

Morecomb Grange.

Arrived at five o'clock to-day.
    Tom saw me safely to the change ;
The carriage met me there half-way ;
    So here I am at Morecomb Grange.

It is a fine old country seat,
    Built in the second Charles' time,
With grace and dignity replete —
    It seems but now just in its prime.

O 2

The stairs are chiefly polish'd oak,
    And all the corridors as well,
But walking on it is no joke,
    For twice to-day I nearly fell.

My room looks down the avenue ;
    And far beyond the chestnut-trees,
There is a most bewitching view,
    That any artist's eye would please.

I am not staying here alone,
    For Clifton's sister, Cousin Jane,
It seems, has come as chaperone—
    I hope and trust she won't remain.

I know we shan't get on at all,
    However hard each of us tries ;
She's dashing, rather dark, thin, tall,
    With cold, keen, piercing light grey eyes.

Grey eyes that read one through and through,
    And find one's weak points out with zest,
That doubt if truth itself is true—
    I like the children much the best !

The eldest boy's away at school,
    A handsome lad, if like his carte ;
A troublesome young dog to rule,
    Old nurse says, though she takes his part.

The next are two precocious girls,
    Just like their mother, I am told,
With masses of soft flaxen curls—
    One twelve, the other ten years old.

Then come two wild young Turks of boys,
    Good friends *we're* safe and sure to be,
In spite of all their pranks and noise,
    For boys take readily to me.

Then there's the " baby," four years old,
    Spoil'd by them all, so much the worse ;
She seems thought worth her weight in gold
    By that fond, fussy old head nurse.

My cousin dined with us at eight,
    Left for the HOUSE at half-past nine,
And—but it's getting very late ;
    I will not write another line.

April 21st.

I've seen the children's pets and toys,
    And help'd Jane in *attempts* to talk ;
Then I, the governess, the boys,
    Baby and nurse, went for a walk.

Nurse is a comely, brisk old dame,
    Who loves the children like her life ;
Just thirty years ago she came,
    Nursemaid to Cousin Clifton's wife.

She married, widow'd in a year,
    Back to her post she went again ;
When Clifton married, she came here,
    And here in state she holds her reign.

The governess is rather shy,
    And holds nurse in the greatest awe ;
While nurse in deference *will* vie,
    And treats Miss Barker's word as law.

'Twould be great fun to watch them both,
    Only one must respect them too,
They seem bound by a solemn oath
    To Clifton's interests to be true.

So each upholds the other's sway,
  For fear the children should rebel ;
To judge from what I saw to-day
  They manage matters pretty well.

They all seem pleased to have me here—
  Not so my worthy Cousin Jane ;
She says, "You find it dull, I fear,"
  As if I wanted to complain !

She is *so* civil and polite,
  In quiet, keep-your-distance style ;
I *hate* those eyes so steely bright,
  I *hate* her calm, contemptuous smile.

It seems, I'm sure I can't tell why,
  As though she were my adverse fate—
I try to bear it pleasantly.
  I do hope Clifton won't be late !

April 22nd.

Jane's husband join'd us here last night,
  A quiet, unassuming man,
Who thinks that all she does is right ;
  I'll imitate him, *if I can.*

We dined, and then I play'd and sang—
　　With Clifton by, I am content.
At ten o'clock the prayer-bell rang ;
　　And that was how the evening went.

April 23rd.   Sunday.
　"　24th.

To-night we'd company to dine,
　　And Clifton was at home by three ;
It may be a mistake of mine,
　　But he does seem so proud of me.

This evening, just as I was dress'd,
　　I heard a voice call, " Cousin Clare !
Papa says, mind you look your best—
　　He's sent some flowers for your hair."

And in the quiet of my room,
　　Where never prying eyes could peep,
I kiss'd the petals' rosy bloom,
　　There Diary ! the secret keep.

April 25th.

A Mr. Reille dined here to-night—
    Jane's husband was detain'd in town ;
As usual, she was full of spite,
    And quite prepared to " set me down."

They had to go up to the House,
    I let them talk away—those three,
And sat still as a little mouse,
    Till Cousin Clifton turn'd to me.

" Well, Clare, what do *you* say ?" and then
    I talk'd, because he liked to hear.
It seem'd to please both gentlemen,
    But Cousin Jane said, with a sneer :

" Twelve years I've been a member's wife,
    And never-heard my husband lay
The law down thus—once in his life,
    As Clare has laid it down to-day.

" But then Charles is a clever man,
    And, like me, hates all false pretence."
" Yes," Clifton said, "the wisest plan,
    For those who can't, like Clare, talk sense."

" Clifton, my dear, you'll turn Clare's head,
    She thinks that compliment is *meant*."
Angrily starting up, he said,
    " Come, Reille ! it is high time we went ;

" The train goes at eighteen past nine ;
    Good evening, Jane ; good evening, Clare ;
What sort of night, Jones ? wet or fine ?
    Come, Reille ! we have no time to spare."

The hall door shut with *such* a bang,
    Jane sigh'd and gently shook her head ;
And then she knitted, and I sang,
    And then we yawn'd, and went to bed.

April 26th.

    ,,   *27th.*

I talk'd of going home to-day,
    But Clifton instantly said " *No*."
So, as he presses, I shall stay—
    For truly I don't want to go.

To see how fond he is of me
    Requires but very little " nous ;"
He's always home to early tea,
    And more than once has shirk'd the House.

Each day is very like the last,
    Breakfast, write letters, luncheon, drive,
Then callers—old, young, slow or fast,
    A yawning fit, and tea at five.

Then Clifton, dinner, music, tea,
    And then a boring talk with Jane.
With him here, time goes joyously,
    But *she* is Pleasure's very bane.

This morning, as we sat at work,
    She ask'd me if I knew Miss White.
I thought I saw a slight smile lurk
    About her mouth—and I was right.

I answer'd " Yes ;" but why should she
    Give her lip that contemptuous curl ?
" A charming girl," she said.   (To me
    She really didn't seem a *girl*.)

" Perhaps she is," was my reply :
    " Extremely self-conceited, too :
It's time she laid girls' graces by
    At her age—thirty-one or two."

And then she look'd me through and through
  With those grey eyes, so keen and cold.
" You thought her *passée*, then, and blue,
  Yet thirty isn't very old."

I felt annoy'd—I don't know why—
  My face flush'd up as hot as hot;
" I didn't like her much," said I ;
  She slightly smiled, " I dare say not."

I hate that cool, contemptuous smile
  That hints, but will not tell outright;
I ask'd her, in a little while,
  " But why should I not like Miss White ? "

" Oh ! have you never heard the tale ?
  Miss White loved Clifton long ago.
But where two strive, the one must fail,
  And he chose Eleanor Defoe.

" And that was a mistake at best—
  Camilla White is more his style.
Ah, well ! poor Eleanor's at rest,
  'Twill come right in a little while.

" Camilla's single, and no doubt
   This time she'll try, and will succeed ;
I'm sure *I'll* try to help her out—
   I wish it from my heart indeed.

" Clever, accomplish'd, she will make
   A wife who well may be his pride ;
I wish it for poor Clifton's sake,
   And those poor children's"—then she sigh'd.

" I think I'll go and smooth my hair ;
   It's nearly lunch time," I replied.
I rush'd up to my room, and there—
   I'm half ashamed to own it !—cried.

April 28*th*.
   „ 29*th*.
   „ 30*th*.
May 1*st*.
   „ 2*nd*.

At last I sit down to record
   The happiest evening of my life ;
A tale of joy —with every word
   With hope and love and longing rife.

Jane and her spouse dined out to-day,
    And, as they were not at home till late,
For once, I had it all my way,
    And dined with Clifton *tête-à-tête*.

Reaching from ceiling to the floor,
    Each side the dining-room, are two
Large mirrors, where one sees twice o'er
    The whole room at a single view.

I sat quite proper and straight-laced,
    While Gregory and Jones were by,
But long'd to see how we look'd, placed
    As master he, as mistress I.

I waited till a good chance came,
    Then glanced—but oh! I felt so wild,
Clifton had done the very same,
    Our eyes met—then I blush'd, he smiled.

" We don't look badly match'd," he said ;
    " I think we could dispense with Jane ;
With you, Clare, at the table-head,
    The old house looks like *home* again."

My heart seem'd suddenly to rise,
  And throb till I could *hear* each beat ;
I did not dare to raise my eyes,
  'Twas almost painful, 'twas so sweet.

I tried to speak—oh ! when did I
  Sit tongue-tied 'gainst my will before ?
I, who am famed for coquetry,
  And count flirtations by the score ?

Speechless, with heart and cheeks aglow,
  I learn'd what real true love is worth ;
'Twas like a dream—I only know
  That Heaven itself seems come to earth.

The spell, however, was but brief,
  For Cousin Clifton spoke again,
And (it was almost a relief)
  This time in quite a different strain.

But in the library alone,
  Waiting for him to come to tea,
I mark'd the softness of the tone
  In which he said those words to me.

Well match'd ! he handsome, stout, and tall,
  With those strong arms and great broad chest ;
And I so delicate and small—
  A wee dove in an eagle's nest.

The hours like minutes seem'd to flee,
  For Time in bliss had steep'd his wings ;
I sang, and then he read to me,
  And then we talk'd of different things.

A vase of early mignonette
  With chasten'd fragrance filled the room ;
We did not talk of love, and yet
  Love seem'd link'd with its soft perfume.

I wonder, as the years roll by,
  If I shall feel most joy or pain,
When, like a flood of memory,
  That scent is borne to me again.

He loves me !—not that he *said* so
  By word or sign, however slight ;
But my heart tells me, for I know
  I ne'er was happy till to-night.
       *   *   *   *   *

Then came a rude awakening shock,
 Just when joy's torch most brightly burn'd,
'Twas the loud double " footman's " knock,
 Which told the Courtenays had return'd.

May 3*rd.*
 , 4*th.*
 „ 5*th.*
Went for our usual drive to-day,
 I thought we chatted rather more,
For Jane was gracious in her way ;
 We got back here at half-past four.

Jones spoke to us as we went through,
 " Miss Seton, ma'am, has been to call ;
And there's a letter, miss, for you—
 It's on the table in the hall."

" What, only one ? " I said, " no more !
 Clifton has plenty, by-the-bye ;"
I turned his over, three or four,
 One, in an instant, caught my eye.

'Twas clearly in a woman's hand,
    What could a woman have to write?
'Twas dainty, scented, monogramm'd
    C. W.—Camilla White!

If there had been a single soul
    At hand just then to whom to speak,
I should have had more self-control,
    And not have been so blindly weak.

But as it was, with Jane so near,
    Whose presence always seems a blight,
I held the letter up, " Look here,"
    I said, " C. W.—Miss White."

" Why not ?" she languidly replied,
    Not looking *at* me, but beyond ;
" 'Tis three years since poor Nellie died,
    So surely they may correspond."

She turn'd, and slowly walk'd away ;
    Slowly I follow'd, with a pain
I never felt before to-day,
    Numbing my very heart and brain.

Oh ! would to God I had not seen
   That hateful letter lying there ;
Yet had I not, there 'twould have been,
   And, after all, why need *I* care ?

May 6th.

  „   *7th. Sunday.*

This evening, just after tea,
   Clifton was sitting by my side,
He jump'd up rather restlessly
   And threw the window open—wide.

'Twas like a warm midsummer night,
   The sky was one dark vault of blue,
And bathed in floods of soft moonlight
   Were lawn and chestnut avenue.

A few stars glitter'd here and there—
   Diana's maidens coy and pale—
And thrilling in the perfumed air,
   The sweet notes of the nightingale.

We all sat listening silently
  To those clear strains' soft rise and fall,
When Clifton whisper'd quietly,
  " Clare, send Eliza for a shawl.

A walk can't hurt you, it's so warm."
  Of course, Jane said I should take cold ;
But, deaf to her, I took his arm,
  Wrapp'd in a shawl, and out we stroll'd.

We saunter'd down the avenue,
  And linger'd talking at the gate ;
I can't think how the moments flew,
  I never guess'd it was so late.

I stood there, fully satisfied,
  Absorb'd in one sweet dream of bliss,
For Clifton drew me to his side,
  And then our lips met in a kiss.

A voice behind us made us start ;
  " Are you not coming in again ? "
I turn'd, and, with a sinking heart,
  Saw Mr. Courtenay and Jane.

How long she'd been there I don't know.
　　But very likely all the time ;
Really, until she told me so,
　　I never thought a walk a crime.

But, shown up in its proper light,
　　Remorse my guilty conscience stings ;
Of course immaculate Miss White
　　Would never do such shocking things.

" Clifton ! how could you loiter so ?
　　Oh ! please come in the shortest way ;
It struck eleven longago !
　　Whatever will the servants say ? "

Thus, and much more, quoth Jane ; we went
　　Back to the house, the prayers were read,
And then " good-night."　I am content ;
　　I hope she is, and now to bed.

May 8th.

As I went to my room to-night,
　　The nursery door was just ajar ;
I heard nurse say, " She and Miss White
　　Are very much upon a par."

I listen'd, then I heard *my* name ;
     Ay, the old proverb's true indeed!
Perhaps, perhaps I was to blame !
     But what I heard made my heart bleed.

" Miss Peyce!" shriek'd nurse, "oh dear ! oh dear !
     I'm sure I hope it's no such thing ;
If a young mistress enters here,
     I know the misery it will bring.

" Those children need such firm control,
     A girl like her will never do ;
Miss White's the best, upon the whole,
     And then they are first cousins too."

" Oh, bother take that !" Susan said,
     " Do let poor master have his way ;
With Miss Peyce at the table-head,
     The old house would be always gay.

" We're not all old, you know, like you ;
     I'd like to have dull times improve ;
You mark my words, you'll find it true,
     Our master's head and ears in love.

" A handsome fellow, too, like him,
  Deserves a handsome wife ; it's clear,
You look so awful cross and grim,
  That you don't want a missus here."

"Oh, Susan ! it is self, self, self,
  And always self with such as you ;
There ! put those books back on the shelf—
  Do something for your living, do !

" It don't become you !   You're too young,
  With master's name to be so free ;
You'll learn, my girl, to hold your tongue,
  When you have lived as long as me.

" It's all but settled with Miss White,
  'Twas Mrs. Courtenay told me *that ;*
But don't talk of it, 'tisn't right,
  To make it food for kitchen chat.

" If Missie makes him change his mind,
  It won't be long afore it's known ;
But if she does, I think she'll find
  She'd better have left well alone.

" If she does marry him, there'll be
　　One wretched heart amongst the lot ;
And that's the master's—deary me !
　　They'd all be wretched, like as not.

" For Missie's a kind-hearted soul,
　　And wouldn't like to be too hard,
And master likes such strict control,
　　That all her projects would be marr'd.

" The children would nigh break her heart ;
　　Then master he'd be harsh and vex'd,
First take hers, then the children's part—
　　We all know what would happen next.

" For all their sakes, I hope he'll find
　　Some one much older than Miss Peyce ;
Some one decided, firm, yet kind,
　　Who'll keep each in their proper place.

" But never Missie—God forbid !
　　She means no harm, I know, not she ;
Young folks don't guess what grief lies hid
　　As long as things look pleasantly.

"She's pretty, ay, a sweeter face
  Ne'er blush'd upon a summer's day;
There's few who wouldn't like Miss Peyce—
  She's lots of sweethearts, I dare say.

"She'll pick up one soon, never fear;
  For, deary, 'twould make my heart sore,
If she should come as mistress here,
  Oh! Susan, speak of it no more.

"I wish I'd died when mistress died,
  If I must ever live to see
Poor little Missie master's bride,
  And hers and master's misery."

I walk'd up here, as in a trance,
  Then flung myself upon the floor,
And o'er my shatter'd sweet romance
  Wept as I never wept before.

Each cruel word was strictly true,
  And *Love* lay stretch'd upon his bier;
What *duty* was, too well I knew,
  Oh! would it were not quite so clear.

Jane's withering sneer and crushing smile,
  My own conviction — which is worse ;
And, as the torch that lights the pile,
  The rambling words of good old nurse.

I'm better now—quite calm again ;
  I've vow'd a solemn vow to-night,
That, though it cause me lifelong pain,
  I'll *force* myself to do the right.

The fearful test may never come,
  And oh ! God grant it never may ;
But soon as can be, I'll go home—
  It is the best, the safest, way.

I'll do my part—but with those words
  All sunshine fades from out my life ;
To breaking stretch'd are my heart's chords !
  Break, if thou wilt, heart, in the strife !

That is not *love*, which grasping takes
  With eager hands love's hoarded pelf ;
The heart that *loves* in anguish breaks,
  Before it gives a thought to self.

Oh! Clifton! Clifton! am I mad?
  No, but I love you more than life.
What matters *my* path being sad,
  If *you* are happy with your wife.

Choose her who is so wise and good ;
  To your old love keep leal and true ;
And, though it costs my heart's best blood,
  'Tis gladly given, Love, for you.

And yet I would that I could die,
  While all my pulses warmly beat,
And, like the swan's one melody,
  Find life's last sighs sublimely sweet.

I've lived till I have tasted *life*,
  I've loved till I am cool and brave ;
And since I cannot be your wife,
  I'll seek my bridal in the grave.

My own, my darling, that one kiss
  My lips for evermore will thrill ;
My heart has sung one psalm of bliss
  Now till eternity 'tis still.

May 9th.

This evening I said to Jane
 'Twas time I bade them all good-bye ;
Clifton still press'd me to remain,
 But I withstood him valiantly.

Jane said in her most dulcet voice,
 "O! really, *must* you run away ?
Clifton, my dear, leave Clare a choice—
 You hear, she doesn't *wish* to stay."

I colour'd up, and so did he —
 I felt so miserably hot ;
Murmur'd mamma was wanting me,
 Or else—oh there! I don't know what.

I know I look'd a perfect fool,
 And Clifton looked annoy'd and vex'd,
And Jane look'd unconcern'd and cool,
 Till I guess'd what would happen next.

She stroked me softly on the cheek,
 "Ah! my wise little Cousin Clare,
No doubt you're wanted home this week—
 There's powerful attraction there.

"The only wonder is, to me,
  How you have kept so long away;
Two letters, eh? an H and G—
  I think they stand for Harold Grey."

Oh! those keen, steely, searching eyes—
  What depths they held of hidden spite!
I said, she saw my temper rise,
  "Did that come from your friend, Miss White?"

She smiled. "Camilla White, my dear,
  Has better work, I hope, to do,
Than send your village gossip here—
  I found the matter out from you."

"From me!" I cried; "I'd almost swear
  I've never mention'd Harold Grey."
She answered, "C'est une autre affaire;
  It isn't what young ladies *say*,

"It's what they hint, and look, and sigh,
  And when they blush, and then turn pale,
That one can read so easily
  A certain interesting tale."

'Twas either Mark Smythe, or his wife,
    Or Miss White, put her up to this ;
I've never blush'd, I'll stake my life —
    I'm no young sentimental miss.

Besides, since I saw Clifton first,
    I've never thought of Harold Grey ;
She knows it, too, and that's the worst,
    Because she sees which card to play.

I tried to argue—'twas in vain,
    She parried everything I said ;
I gave it up, and once again
    I wish'd at heart that I was dead.

But two days will pass quickly by,
    And when I'm once at home again
I'll learn to struggle patiently
    With this dull load of secret pain.

It was a king among kingly trees,
An oak whose branches stretch'd far and wide.
And a butterfly flew in light-hearted ease
And sunn'd herself where herself did please,
Or shelter'd her wings 'neath his stately pride.

But there came a torrent of thunder rain
And the butterfly's painted wings were furl'd,
For never more she could fly again.
Alas ! for the hearts that are drown'd in pain,
There are some such in God's beautiful world.

May 10*th.*

„   11*th.*

„   12*th.*

How can I write with thoughts astray ?
    How can I write with heart grown cold ?
And yet the tale of yesterday,
    My life's great epoch, *must* be told.

Jane went out for her usual drive,
    I said I'd go—then changed my mind ;
Clifton was *never* home till five,
    So I might safely stay behind.

I told her that I had to pack,
    It was but an excuse, I own,
I meant to sit, till she came back ;
    In the old library—*alone.*

I tried to read—my throbbing brain
    Refused to grasp the simplest theme ;
I tried to write—'twas all in vain,
    It seem'd like writing in a dream.

Restless and sad, I fetch'd my work—
    The clock had just chimed half-past three,
When the door open'd with a jerk—
    Clifton stood face to face with me !

" Well, Clare," he said, " I'm tired of town,
    I thought you wouldn't drive to-day ;
Jane's out of course—that's well—sit down,
    I've something, dear, I want to say."

It had been coming long, I knew,
    And now at length the time had come ;
There were no others save us two,
    And he spoke on, and I was dumb.

'Twas quickly said—he did not waste
    The words that made my pale cheeks burn
Besides, he said, he spoke in haste,
    Fearing that Jane might soon return.

Each syllable he utter'd fell
  Like living fire upon my heart,
But I had school'd myself too well
  To falter with my bitter part.

"I build my hopes, dear Clare," he said,
  "On all that pass'd the other night;"
So then I laugh'd, and toss'd my head,
  And ask'd him—how about Miss White?

I wish'd to make him think I chose
  To treat the matter as a joke;
He bit his lips, his colour rose,
  And for a second neither spoke.

At last he said, "I'll tell the truth,
  Miss White has loved me, Clare, for years:
For love of me she spent her youth
  In unavailing sighs and tears;

"For love of me she's single yet,
  From her heart's shrine she could not tear
The lover she will ne'er forget,
  And place another idol there.

" Words cannot tell her kindness when
　　Poor Eleanor fell ill and died ;
I must have been the worst of men
　　If I had not felt gratified.

" Since then Jane told me all her tale,
　　And as I once again was free,
I felt this time I must not fail
　　The one who'd loved so patiently.

" She's brilliant, clever, and well-read,
　　Just in her prime at thirty-three,
A splendid figure, lovely head,
　　And more than all—she's fond of me !

" As yet the offer's but *implied*—
　　I've drawn up, but not sign'd the bond ;
Although, to keep her satisfied,
　　At intervals we correspond.

" In *honour*, Clare, I'm bound to keep
　　To my implied gage staunch and true ;
But honour's guard is lull'd asleep
　　If I but turn to *look* at you.

" In your hands lies my future life.
  For Honour fails with Love to cope ;
Camilla cannot be my wife
  Till you deny a gleam of hope.

" But if you love me, darling, *speak*—
  The promise I have made to her
Is not so binding but 'twill break."
  He paused ; my heart was all astir.

My brain whirl'd round, and in my ear
  I heard old nurse's accents ring—
" If a young mistress enters here,
  I know the misery it will bring.

" Those children need such strict control."
  I knew—I felt the bitter truth,
And in my very inmost soul
  I cursed the only bar—my youth.

I could not speak ; he spoke again :
  " Clare, dear, I wait for your reply."
And then I answer'd, mad with pain,
  (Oh ! God forgive me for the lie) :—

CLARE PEYCE'S DIARY.

" I cannot love you "—'twas the best,
    The best for him, the best for all ;
I felt it was—but in my breast
    All happiness seem'd turn'd to gall.

He answer'd something, but I dared
    Not listen, for he pleaded hard ;
Nor he nor I that hour I spared,
    Though all my life by it was marr'd.

I closed my ears to what he said,
    Crush'd down my foolish aching heart,
I curl'd my lip and toss'd my head,
    Right cleverly I play'd my part !

At last he took my trembling hand.
    " Clare ! once again I bid you choose,
And let me clearly understand—
    Do you accept me or refuse ? "

I smiled, and tried to smile in scorn.
    " If e'er I marry, it must be
A man rich, handsome, and well-born
    But—only twenty-two or three."
He winced ; I saw he felt the thorn,
    It was some comfort—*that*—to me.

He look'd me through, and through, and through —
    One minute more, I should have cried,
" Oh ! Clifton, darling, I love *you*,
    Far more than all the world beside."

But not another word said he,
    And so that searching look I braved ;
And then he left me, silently,
    And thus his happiness was saved !

'Twas done. Deliberately I wrought
    The deed that crush'd my future life.
Lost seem'd existence in the thought
    I never now can be his wife !

I follow'd him as in a dream—
    The room seem'd whirling round and round—
Strange lights seem'd dazzlingly to gleam ;
    I walk'd, but did not feel the ground.

I did not cry, I had no tears,
    I have none now—their silent balm
Lies hidden in far future years ;
    But now, oh ! I am very calm.

'Twas not so dreadful as I fear'd,
  From my heart's gash the life-blood stream'd ;
But now with red-hot iron 'tis sear'd,
  And it is only deeply seam'd.

The danger's over—it is done !
  And, let me rue it as I may,
The battle's fought, the victory won—
  I cannot call back yesterday.

Clifton has not been home to-night ;
  To-morrow by an early train
I leave, and then Camilla White
  May choose her wedding-dress with Jane.

God bless them both ! my every prayer
  Asks blessings on their future life.
God bless their footsteps everywhere !
  " Miss White " is lost in " Clifton's wife."

May 20th.   Sevenoaks.

I have been home a week to-day,
  A week since my heart's tale was closed ;
This very morning Harold Grey
  Met me out walking, and proposed.

I pitied him as I said "No!"
   Just "no," for I could say no more ;
'Tis such a little while ago
   That I that bitter anguish bore.

He said that I had changed my mind,
   He thought *I* was above caprice ;
I tried my utmost to be kind,
   But fail'd, and failing held my peace. ·

I had no spirits to say much,
   For gathering tears my eyes made dim ;
But held my hand out, and its touch
   Told more than words I grieved for him.

We understood each other then,
   For as we stood there, hand in hand,
He said, " Ah ! Clare, I ask'd *since when*
   You'd changed, but now I understand.

" I should have spoken long ago,
   'Tis my own folly I've to blame ;
You won't quite cut me."   " Oh ! no, no !
   We'll be friends always just the same."

And so we parted, each love crush'd,
   Each heart with its best angel flown;
Not happy lovers, proud and flush'd,
   But sadden'd, hopeless, and alone.

Oh! hearts that daily throb and beat
   With all lost that made *living, life,*
Not daring to call memory sweet,
   Teach me how best to bear the strife!

May 27th.

Another week has pass'd away!
   I have no heart for anything,
Existence drags on day by day—
   I hate these sunny days of spring.

All Nature wakes to life and light,
   Rejoicing; I alone repine;
The flowers forget their wintry night—
   I only live to dwell on mine.

Oh would, oh would that I were dead,
   Far from repining grief and pain!
Lay down to-night my weary head,
   And never wake on earth again.

They say I'm paler every day,
   Mamma is very, very kind,
Papa says, in his joking way,
   "Why, Clare! you've left your heart behind."

They dose with iron and quinine,
   Port wine and jelly, say the spring
Is trying, talk of change of scene,
   Excitement, and that kind of thing.

No one, I'm sure, suspects the truth,
   Unless our doctor's practised eye
Has caught a something that mere youth
   And trying springs don't justify.

"Don't fidget her," he said one day,
   "It's simply nerves, there's nothing wrong ;
Just pet her, give her her own way,
   She'll be all right again ere long."

June 14th.

As we were breakfasting to-day,
   Mamma remark'd the post was late ;
"Oh! no!" said Tom, "he's been our way,
   I saw a letter on Clare's plate.

"You should have seen her snatch it up;"
    Just then I caught my father's eye,
My hand shook, I upset my cup,
    And stammer'd "I'll explain by-and-by."

"Be quiet, Tom, and do not tease,"
    Mamma said; "let your sister be."
At last I gain'd my room in peace
    To read what he has said to me.

A wild, vague hope, I know, I nursed,
    And with it too a sickening fear;
At last I broke the seal; for worst
    Or best I knew my fate was here!

For no mere trivial cause he'd write;
    Whate'er it be to Fate I bow.
'Tis as I thought—Camilla White
    Is his betroth'd; all's over now.

He writes: "I made a great mistake
    To dream you'd ever fancy me;
Your heart is hardly wide awake,
    And mine told out to forty-three.

" It was a foolish dream of mine ;
    Forgive, forget it, Cousin Clare ;
Forgive, forget, and write a line
    To say we are the friends we were.

" And if you ever need a friend
    To help or serve you *any* way,
Remember you have but to send,
    And I'll be with you, night or day.

" My last request was wild, 'tis true ;
    But friendship you can freely take ;
Take, then, what I now offer you,
    For my and for Camilla's sake."

He never loved as I have loved !
    He could not, thus to write to me !
So cold, so satisfied, unmoved,
    Could *I?* with all my misery.

She has his *heart*, his *fancy* I,
    And he has both our very lives—
A fair exchange ! Society
    Would scarcely sanction both as wives.

Yet why be bitter?　It is best
　To dash the past at once aside,
And tear for ever from my breast
　The sting of disappointed pride.

His friend! ah, yes! his wounded pride,
　The rankling darts Love leaves behind ;
His brilliant hopes, his stylish bride,
　Could never make him aught but kind.

His friend ! ah, yes ! in life and death ;
　Nay more than death—eternity ;
No more nor less by one hair's breadth,
　Just friend, and only friend, to me.

He is the wisest ! till life ends
　We're knit by a new sacred tie ;
Love is forgotten, trusted *friends*
　We'll meet, without regret or sigh.

June 18th.

The news has very quickly spread ;
　This afternoon Tom met Miss White ;
He says he's sure it's turn'd her head,
　She was so radiant with delight.

Radiant! why all that life can hold
  Is pour'd into her willing hands ;
And Love has woven a web of gold,
  With diamond woof and sunshine strands.

Sorrow for her can never come,
  Or come robb'd of its sharpest sting ;
His wife! *his* darling ! peace and home—
  Radiant ! why, she has everything.

And I ? I might have had it all,
  Yet I have acted for the best ;
The crumbs at least to my share fall,
  For by my hand two lives are blest.

Be still, my heart ! nor dare repine,
  One grand sweet solace ne'er forget :
'Twas for his peace I barter'd mine—
  That leaves no room for vain regret !

August 17th.

Two months ago since I wrote last !
  The wedding's over ; they will soon
(Time flies on such swift pinions past)
  Be finishing their honeymoon.

Next week they are expected home,
    And Jane has gone down to prepare ;
The boys write word they are to come,
    And thus all meet together there.

Wife, children, sister ! one and all—
    How happy they'll that evening be !
Will any idle word recall
    A single memory of me ?

Ah ! better not, perhaps, for him !
    Regret and joy are strangely blent ;
May God fill his cup to the brim
    With happiness—mine with content.

I would not change the lot I chose
    With any loved and loving wife ;
My heart its own deep secret knows,
    One golden thread runs through my life.

A box of summer mignonette
    Sends its soft fragrance through the room ;
Old memories crowd its message, yet
    They're memories sweet as its perfume.

August 30th.   Morecomb Grange.

How I have lived throughout to-day,
  And yet have strength to think and write,
I know not ; all seems far away—
  A dream that's haunting me to-night.

A wild, weird dream of anguish'd pain—
  Too sudden, awful, to be true—
That comes again and yet again,
  With Truth's wan features peering through.

I cannot sit down still and weep—
  Tears are no solace for such pain ;
They've left me, as they say, to sleep—
  Sleep ! with this throbbing heart and brain.

I dare not *think*, I'll try to write
  The agony of this day's tale ;
But what my heart must bear to-night
  I cannot write, for words would fail.

This morning (I was quite alone)
  A telegram was brought to me ;
I saw 'twas urgent from its tone—
  " A train leaves yours at ten to three.

"Clifton is ill—be sure to come."
　　A second follow'd on the first ;
It ran, "Set out at once from home,"
　　And then I fear'd the very worst.

But how I left, how I came here,
　　I hardly know—I hardly knew ;
My very soul was sick with fear
　　As I drove up the avenue.

The house look'd wretched in its state,
　　The avenue was spread with straw.
Oh God ! if I have come too late !
　　I thought, with horror-stricken awe.

The door was open'd ere I knock'd,
　　"Oh miss!" said Jones, "thank God, you're here.
He's much the same—oh ! weren't you shock'd ?
　　It's merciful it happen'd near.

" He is amongst us all at last,
　　Poor gentleman ; we'll see him die.
We all thought once—ah ! well, that's past.
　　There ! there ! Miss Peyce, you mustn't cry.

"You know about it all, of course—
    What! not a word?" thus on he ran,
And made me listen by sheer force,
    Poor, honest, garrulous old man.

It seems some horses ran away
    And, dashing round a corner, threw
Camilla down, or so they say,
    For *how* it happen'd no one knew.

He caught the horses by the rein,
    And saved his wife! *how*, none can tell;
Ere he could free himself again,
    His hand gave way—he slipp'd and fell.

Off tore the horses at full speed,
    Wildly and madly on their way;
Camilla stood from danger freed—
    Insensible and crush'd he lay!

Her life was bought with his.   In vain
    I gave my heart's best hopes to save
His life from sorrow, grief, or pain—
    My very care has dug his grave.

" Who was it sent for me ?" I ask'd.
    " Oh ! missus wanted long ago
(Poor soul !   She's downright overtask'd) ;
    But Mrs. Courtenay, she said *No.*

" All yesterday he raved of you ;
    He wander'd very much towards night ;
But sometimes he was conscious too,
    And begg'd of missus so to write.

" This morning he's as clear as clear,
    And asked so piteous if they'd sent,
That missus said you'd soon be here,
    And then, poor dear, he seem'd content."

" Is that Miss Peyce, Jones ?" said a voice.
    " I fear I hurried you to-day ;
But life and death admit no choice—
    In his state one dare not delay."

Haggard and wan, with swollen eyes,
    Shorn of each insolence and grace,
I gazed at her in mute surprise !
    It could *not* be Camilla's face !

" Poor girl ! how ill you look," she said.
  " This trouble has aged you by years."
" Is there *no* hope ? " She shook her head,
  And burst into a flood of tears.

I let her weep, my tears were dry ;
  But hers were a relief, I knew.
She roused herself up, by-and-bye,
  "Oh dear ! I never thought of you.

" There's luncheon laid, come in with me."
  " I couldn't eat." " Ay, but you must :
Just try, 'tis a necessity—
  A glass of sherry and a crust.

" He's sleeping now, you cannot go
  Until he wakes up once again :
Do come with me, you need it so.
  Who's that ? oh ! it's only Jane."

Jane, too, look'd worn, but she was cold,
  As if her heart was made of stone ;
She greeted me just as of old,
  And ask'd me if I came alone.

" My brother somehow wish'd for you,"
   She went on frigidly to say ;
" He wanders rather "—then I knew
   She meant he wander'd yesterday.

" My dear Camilla, do lie down,
   You're quite worn out—I'll see to Clare ;
The doctors won't be here from town
   Till half-past four—you've time to spare."

" I cannot rest," Camilla said,
   In such a weary, heart-sick tone ;
" I'll come with you, my heart's like lead —
   I cannot bear to be alone."

That luncheon was a wretched meal ;
   Each bore up for the other's sake ;
Each feign'd a calm she did not feel,
   Then nurse said Clifton was awake.

The few words seem'd to pierce my heart,
   I gave a sort of gasping sigh ;
Thus surely the condemn'd must start,
   The hour they are led forth to die.

" Come with me, Clare," Camilla said
    (She never call'd me " Clare " before) ;
" Tread lightly, dear, it hurts his head,
    Our very step across the floor."

Before we reach'd his room she paused,
    And took me gently in her arms ;
" Ah ! Clare," she said, " we've often caused
    Each other jealous, vague alarms.

" But try to love me, *for his sake,*
    You're his in heart, if I'm in name ;
This trouble all old piques must break—
    In grief, poor child, we are the same."

Tears choked my answer, but I threw
    My arms around her, closely press'd
My hated rival, and I knew
    She felt all I'd have fain express'd.

Pushing the door with cautious touch,
    And hardly breathing, in we crept ;
Oh God ! we've loved him far too much :
    Our idol from its shrine is swept.

The servants hush'd, and white with fear,
  The house so silent in its gloom,
All spoke Death's presence very near,
  But more than all, this darken'd room.

A few rays of the August sun,
  Stole stealthily along the floor ;
Emblems of life with bliss o'errun,
  But now shut out for evermore.

White as the sheets, and rack'd with pain,
  Helpless as any new-born child,
Lay Clifton, but 'twas not in vain
  I'd come, he knew me and he smiled.

"Dearest," Camilla said, "here's Clare,
  "I think you'd like to be alone ;"
And then, before I was aware,
  She kiss'd me lightly, and was gone.

And then! ah! there was no disguise—
  The time for all disguise had pass'd ;
We look'd into each other's eyes,
  And knew and felt the truth at last.

"Then you did love me, little Clare?
  My darling! say so in this hour,
When life has so few sands to spare,
  This world's temptations no more power."

And as the rock at Moses' rod
  In streams of living water gush'd,
So to the dying and our God,
  Forth from my heart my secret rush'd.

"Loved you! oh! Clifton, 'twas for you
  I gave up all that made life sweet;
Glad to be thought unkind, untrue,
  To fling life's treasures at your feet.

"I was not fit to be your wife,
  And so, my love, I stood aside,
Thinking by that to crown your life
  With one so suited for your bride."

"Kiss me, then, darling, once again,
  Oh! do not grieve so for me, Clare;
'Tis for the best,"—he stopp'd, for Jane,
  Nurse, and Camilla all stood there.

The darken'd room, their cautious tread,
Had brought them on us by surprise,
Until they stood beside the bed—
Jane's wrath was flashing from her eyes.

" Camilla, dear," she cried, "don't stay ;
This scene is terrible for you ;
Let me implore you, come away,"
While poor nurse call'd out, "Hush, ma'am, do."

But, with her arm fast round me thrown,
Camilla said, " I see all, dear.
Do make them leave us quite alone—
Only we three are wanted here."

Then, almost in its usual tone,
The words rang out so strong and plain,
Clifton said, " Leave us quite alone,
We want no interference, Jane."

She knew she dared not disobey,
For any scene might cause his death ;
Trembling with rage, she went away,
Muttering, " For shame !" below her breath.

And we two knelt there, side by side,
  Each losing with *him* all of life,
Each to be near *him* satisfied,
  Forgotten rivalry and strife.

Loving too deeply for a thought
  Of self, or selfish grief to rise,
By one strong bond together brought,
  In one strong cause to sympathize.

Into her hands his love I pour'd,
  Because for *him*—I deem'd it best ;
Back to my heart she has restored
  That love, to give *his* spirit rest.

His happiness we seek, not ours,
  And, knit by a new solemn tie,
I see in these last precious hours,
  She loved as faithfully as I.

We knelt some time in silence there,
  Then Clifton gave a hand to each,
" Poor little wife—poor little Clare,"
  He said in faltering, feeble speech.

" You must not grieve like this for me,
    Both of you love me far too well ;
Two nobler hearts can never be
    Than those I'm forced to bid farewell.

" Camilla, dear one, take my hand,
    And let me hear you truly say
That you forgive, and understand
    All that you saw and heard to-day."

" Forgive ! " she said, " my whole heart aches
    For that poor child's grief-clouded life ;
For even if mine with sorrow breaks,
    At least, at least, I've been your wife.

" Those few bright weeks of love and bliss,
    No future grief can take away ;
It is enough, I lived for this,
    It was too glorious to stay.

" You thought me worthy of your home,
    Your trust, your confidence, esteem ;
As years roll'd on, love might have come,
    And realized my girlhood's dream.

" But oh ! my husband, my heart's blood
    I'd give, just once to hear you say,
Had you been spared, you *might* have loved,
    As you have loved Clare Peyce to-day."

Then as she bent her face to his,
    He kiss'd her, stroked her poor pale brow,
And whisper'd, " *Life* brought nought like this,
    I never loved you, sweet, *till now.*"

I did not grudge her that, oh ! *no.*
    What ! grudge balm to a breaking heart :
My tears began at once to flow,
    But 'twas her sorrow made them start.

I felt no longer I dare stay,
    Hers were the last few threads of life ;
I kiss'd them, softly stole away,
    And left the husband and the wife.

TEN YEARS AFTER.

Sevenoaks.   June 19th.

JUST twenty-nine to-day!   Ah me!
   I see some grey amongst my hair ;
And know I never more can be
   The belle they vaunted everywhere.

I've read the diary I kept
   In those old days – ten years ago ;
Not that its memories have slept,
   But Time must heal the sharpest woe.

Camilla is a widow still,
   But will not be one long, they say ;
" Who's tapping at my window-sill ? "
   A tiny voice says, " Hawold Gwey."

" Come in, my godson !   What ! all those
   Bright golden buttercups for me ;
A pansy, and a China rose,
   A dandelion, and sweet pea.

"A note from mother, too!" She says,
  "Dear Clare, my brother Fred is here;
He's always raving in your praise,
  Do come and meet him, like a dear."

"Now Harold, pet, run off and say,
  Godmother's love, but she's afraid
She cannot come across to-day,
  And that she is a sworn old maid."

Off speeds my messenger—I know
  His errand will be truly done;
My heart flies back to long ago,
  Clifton! *I* have no loves but one.

AS LIFE ITSELF.

DEDICATION.

My husband! when God join'd our hands,
  For halcyon days or cloudy weather,
Of roses were the welcome bands
  Which bound our wedded hearts together.

If thorns should spring up here and there,
  When sorrow's touch the fact discloses,
That, though Love shield with watchful care,
  Life's path is never all of roses—

We'll cling the closer, dear, and say
  Tears are but dew-drops joys adorning;
For many a radiant summer day
  Has followed on a rainy morning.

One grief on us can never fall,
  By one cloud ne'er our home be blighted;
For each to each is all in all,
  And love by love is well requited.

Then, since a thought of yours or mine
  Is but half blest unless 'tis " ours,"
Accept the fancies which entwine
  Your wife's day-dreams in idle hours.

AS LIFE ITSELF.

———◆———

PART I.

SUNLIGHT.

⌇⌇⌇⌇⌇⌇

FERNBROOK.

JULY! a July afternoon!
   The sun bakes up the country street.
And panting Nature seems to swoon
   With the intensity of heat.

The dogs lie basking in the sun;
   The children loiter in their play,
And leave a game but just begun
   With "Oh! it is *too* hot to-day."

s 2

The scene one may see anywhere—
　　The dull scene of a country town :
Windows wide open for the air,
　　Venetian blinds drawn closely down.

One house is larger than the rest—
　　It stands back somewhat from the street—
And looks a sweet old-fashion'd nest
　　Where ease and comfort are complete.

Shut in by noble chestnut-trees,
　　The solid red brick seems to say,
" Choose modern houses, ye who please ;
　　I was not run up yesterday."

The tendrils of the jessamine
　　About the gables twine and rest,
Its pure and fragrant blossoms shine
　　Like stars upon a hero's breast.

A lawn slopes to the river's brink,
　　Which parts the garden from the fields,
Where thirsty cattle stoop to drink ;
　　And peace the whole fair picture shields.

But truly if walls did have ears,
  And doors all that they heard could tell,
From out the history of years
  Some brave old yarns that house might spell.

There Cavaliers, in Cromwell's day,
  With red wine made the bumpers gleam,
And held their cups (so legends say)
  Above the river's silver stream.

There hunted Royalists have fled
  For safety from pursuer's knife ;
There noble hearts to death have bled
  For country's wrongs and party strife.

There many a gay carouse was held ;
  There lands changed masters in a trice ;
And gold was lost, and oaks were fell'd,
  By one throw of the gamer's dice.

But centuries have pass'd since then,
  And times and scenes have sober'd down :
Those gallants wild, and daring men,
  Would scarcely suit our quiet town.

The doctor's daughters, lawyer's wife,
   And banker's sons would look aghast
At those mad scenes of mirth or strife,
   And cut them as " by far too fast."

Then at their billiards or their tea
   Would talk the scandal of the day ;
And no wise-judging Pharisee
   Would have such charity as they.

Oh ! charming little country cliques !
   Who know each point where each one fails ;
Made up of jealous pride and piques,
   Of envious tattle, idle tales ;

Feeding upon yourselves, until
   Your minds are narrow as your sphere ;
Cramping all liberty of will
   Or thought by " Do as *we* do here."

That your one way was never mine,
   Nor my way yours, is very plain.
But—it is time to draw the line—
   Back to the old red house again.

The door stands open.   Cross the hall :
    That is the dining-room—just peep.
Is any one in there at all ?
    Only a lady, fast asleep.

A dear old dame with snowy hair ;
    A grand old dame, who might have been
An empress in her easy chair,
    If crowns were won by looks and mien.

And never empress yet possess'd
    More love of sovereign power than she.
But softly !—leave her to her rest ;
    We'll see what else there is to see.

The garden has a vagrant grace ;
    Its plants and bushes, scarcely train'd,
Just straggle all about the place,
    By landscape-gardeners unrestrain'd.

The hollyhock and columbine,
    Sweetwilliam, marigold, and pink
Their sweet old-fashion'd charms combine ;
    And wild flowers deck the river-brink.

Down the broad gravel path we'll find
　The shady nooks beside the stream,
Where one might lie for hours reclined
　To watch the sparkling bubbles gleam,

As bright gem-tinted dragon-flies
　Skim humming through the scented grass,
Or lazy trout, stirr'd to surprise,
　Start as some hurrying footsteps pass.

Now comes the orchard ; and just here
　A quiet haunt where none can pry—
The sort of haunt to lovers dear,
　Secure from every curious eye.

The trunks of two huge chestnut-trees
　Support a rustic garden-seat,
Inviting one to dreamy ease,
　Safe shelter'd from the scorching heat.

The branches, bending to the ground,
　An arbour of themselves have made ;
And on the sultriest days are found,
　Beneath their leaves, cool rest and shade.

Two lovers seek that shelter now—
    And let not wiser heads condemn
If broad green leaf and sturdy bough
    Shut in an Eden world for them.

They form a pretty picture there !
    The girl's white dress and bright young face ;
The youth—tall, muscular, and fair—
    With more of power than of grace.

She holds some flowers in her hand,
    And parts the branches as she throws,
As far as may be from the land,
    For each of them a crimson rose.

" See, Will ! " she says, " away they glide ! "
    But, oh ! her face has clouded o'er ;
" They are not floating side by side ;
    Look, Will ! ah ! they have join'd once more ! "

They watch the roses out of sight ;
    Then, blushing in her girlish glee,
She laughs, " Ah, Will, the omen's right ;
    I'm true, if you are true to me."

What does he answer ?   Need one say ?
  Small need to paint a scene like this ;
Such things are happening every day,
  When lips are red and sweet to kiss.

And that Will found them very sweet
  May be premised from his reply ;
For, now the picture is complete,
  I'll name the lovers—Will and I.

  Where the honeysuckle, straying
    In amongst the reeds and grasses,
  With the willow herb is playing,
    And the west wind as he passes
  Stoops awhile and sighs and lingers,
  Kissing her soft, rosy fingers :

  Where grave aconites blue-hooded
    And tall lilies white and stately
  Peep through hedgerows thickly wooded
    At the nuts, and smile sedately—
  There my love and I together
  Laugh at aught save summer weather.

We met in this way : from a child
  I lived with "grannie," at The Lees ;
I think I grew up rather wild,
  With no one but myself to please.

For grandmamma, whose rigid law
  No son nor daughter could relax,
Who kept her world in wholesome awe,
  To me was pliable as wax.

And thus I was, at seventeen,
  As wild and wilful as the wind ;
Ah ! when I think of what has been,
  Those days seem very far behind.

Though grandmamma went rarely out,
  Yet I went everywhere ; you see,
She thought girls ought to go about,
  And any one took charge of me.

One night—'twas at the county ball
  I saw Will first—my heart was light ;
I laugh'd, coquetted, danced with all,
  Nor dreamt that gayest flowers may blight.

The usual county set was there—
  Good-natured, fox-hunting papas ;
And girls, brought like the sheep to fair
  By buxom, whist-loving mammas ;

Young matrons, blooming as a rose,
  Who'd " done " this ball year after year,
Proud to relate how Johnnie grows,
  And the new baby's " such a dear ! "

Spinsters who've touch'd the shady side
  Of—(never mind)—but still are young,
And, envious of the latest bride,
  To every bachelor give tongue.

A sprinkling of the London " swells,"
  Who superciliously survey
The country charms of local belles,
  Pure Sèvres criticizing clay !

And young men cluster'd in a knot,
  Friends, brothers, cousins, kith and kin,
As they observe, " The Fernbrook lot,
  With one or two new-comers in."

Which means the ball is in *their* eyes
The very thing—*crème de la crème*—
Since Fernbrook is a paradise,
Themselves perfection's other name.

This was the sort of thing one heard—
The scraps of talk I used to catch—
" They'd best take care, upon my word,
Or, you see, it will be a match."

" Yes, passable—her looks won't last."
" Call'd ! ! ! nay, not I—who *are* they, pray ? "
" I'm told he's really *very* fast."
" Oh ! lovely ! that cerise and grey ! "

" Well, I heard from the fountain-head
She isn't left a single sou."
" My dear, I live in daily dread :
What next will servants want to do ? "

" I don't think much of Dacre's wine."
" Yes, just the set one's sure to meet."
" I fear he's in a deep decline."
" This weather's ruining the wheat."

"Ah ! yes—no doubt—still it *is* thought—"
  " They tell me Featherstone won't bet."
" I hear his sermons all are bought."
  " I haven't found a coachman yet."

" Yes, we come up to town next year."
  " How charmingly that dress is made ! "
" Well, I don't care if they *do* hear—
  That rubber was *not* fairly play'd."

Will was a perfect godsend then,
  So clever, witty, and well-bred ;
Used as I was to stupid men,
  No wonder that he turn'd my head.

The others were annoy'd and hurt,
  Complain'd I cut them all that night,
Declared I was an arrant flirt—
  No heart so false, no eyes so bright.

I felt the room had Argus eyes,
  And every eye was bent on us ;
That girls all envied me my prize,
  And matrons meant to " make a fuss."

As we were sitting on the stairs,
　I heard old Lady Maltmash say,
" 'Tis true, 'tis not my place, but theirs—
　Still, going on in *such* a way,

" I really ought to interfere."
　Another voice said, " Let them be ;
It's quite correct—*I* brought him here ;
　He's grandson to old Pettigree."
　　*　　*　　*　　*　　*
I loved him—ay, with all my heart,
　But knew not then what real love meant ;
Only a fountain seem'd to start
　With sparkling waters of content.

Enough for me, the fountain's spray
　Was rainbow-tinted ; I'd not found
How deep the hidden sources lay
　Within my very heart-strings wound.

Some whisper'd he was fast and wild,
　Reckless and sensual—what cared I ?
At every hint I calmly smiled,
　Secure in my idolatry.

And yet it vex'd me when Will seem'd
  So callous when compared with some :
Was this the lover I had dream'd
  All in good time would surely come ?

Why should he make so sure of me ?
  I need not marry him perforce ;
Why take my love so quietly ?
  All things to him were things of course.

Our curate was a handsome man,
  Not long from college : when he came
The Fernbrook girls at once began
  To angle for a change of name.

He proved High Church : they one and all
  The daily service never miss'd ;
And gave up picnic, dance, or ball,
  At decorations to assist.

They wore black faithfully all Lent,
  Took classes at the Sunday-school ;
And round their districts bravely went,
  With ardour no repulse could cool.

But I did nothing of all this :
　　It was not that I did not care ;
But one seems all the good to miss
　　When interest has so large a share.

Oh, dear me ! how I was run down !
　　I thought but of this world—no more :
Yet somehow in our little town
　　None loved me better than the poor.

One lone old widow used to say,
　　" They comes with those there little tracts,
And talks and talks ; but you, Miss May,
　　You are the one as comes and *acts*."

Poor soul—'twas little I had done ;
　　Some flowers for her window-sill—
May-be a shilling for her son
　　When he was out of work and ill.

Another woman said to me,
　　" My master says, if it was you,
He'd stand their visits willingly ;
　　And that's what *he'd* say of but few.

"We ain't forgotten little Jack,
    And how you'd bring him toys and books,
To keep him quiet on his back :
    He's strong now, miss, for all his looks."

And one man, bent and good for nought,
    Would give his dim old eyes a wipe,
And think the "baccy" that I brought
    Almost too good for earthly pipe.

So, though I was not on his staff,
    Our curate often heard my name ;
And many a time he'd joke and laugh,
    And say the praise outweigh'd the blame.

At length *his* praise grew very warm—
    His calls more frequent, and his stay
More lengthen'd, till it grew a form
    To visit grannie *every* day.

The dear old lady, shrewd and wise
    In other things, to this was blind ;
She look'd on him with partial eyes,
    And merely thought him—very kind.

I never had a thought of harm,
    Nor do I really think had he ;
But Will's quick temper took alarm,
    Half furious with jealousy.

" May ! I have had enough of this ;
    Suspicion's certainty with me :
If you are tired of me—one kiss ;
    I'm off at once, and you are free.

" But as for that black, sneaking cur,
    Who's taken one I held so dear,
He shall account to me for her—
    A parson's coat's no safeguard here."

Said I, " I don't know what you mean ;
    You needn't be so much enraged,
Nor set to work to make a scene :
    Of course he knows that I'm engaged."

" Of course he does," was his reply ;
    " And, knowing that, more scoundrel he
To haunt the place when I'm not by,
    To try and steal a march on me.

" But there, you clearly like him best :
    Take him at once, in heaven's name ;
I've only been an idle jest
    Since first the simpering idiot came.

" But then, of course, my eyes aren't blue,
    Nor my hair all in little curls ;
I wouldn't though, if I were you,
    Let him confess too many girls.

" He might serve you as you've served me ;
    Men even sometimes change their mind ;
A sneak once, always sneak will be."
    " Thank you," said I, " you're very kind."

Then came a long and sulky pause :
    He laid one hand upon my chair,
And said, " I don't speak without cause :
    Come, May, confess—'tis only fair."

But I was angry too, and gave
    My head a most contemptuous toss ;
Inform'd him I was not his slave,
    He'd best go elsewhere to be cross.

" Do you mean quarrelling ? " he said ;
  " Tell me, at least, what *do* you mean ? "
And then I turn'd away my head—
  " I tell you I don't want ' a scene.'

" Go ! if that's what you want to do ;
  I'm sure I don't care how it ends :
I'm really tired to death of you,
  For ever grumbling at my friends."

" If I go *now*," he said, " I go
  For good, so you've but to decide."
He spoke deliberately and low ;
  I shrugg'd my shoulders and replied,—

" You've lately been so cold and cross,
  If you're not better soon, I'm sure
Your going will not be much loss."
  But I'd said more than he'd endure.

" You think so, May ! I'll never stoop
  To ask you to take back *that* speech ;
I see I've been the fool and dupe ;
  I've learnt the lesson you would teach.

" I wish you good-bye now, and hope
  The Reverend Horace Jasper Vaughan,
With surplice, cassock, alb, and cope,
  Will suit *exactly*—when I'm gone."

That was the parting shot he cast ;
  We met next week estranged and cold,
Just bowing slightly as we pass'd—
  The play play'd out, the story told.

Fernbrook, delighted, had a score
  Of different versions of the tale :
" 'Twas what they'd all been looking for ;
  Such long engagements always fail."

The men blamed him, the girls blamed me ;
  Aunt Anne declared her mind was eased,
She'd often warn'd me how 'twould be —
  Of course men won't stand being teased.

None knew the burning tears that fell
  When ring and letters were return'd ;
No one from my light words could tell
  How my whole nature grieved and yearn'd.

I thought 'twas easy work to part,
   And little guess'd the bitter pain—
The trouble that would rend my heart
   When our two lives were *really* twain.

The dull, long autumn pass'd at length—
   We never heard a word of Will ;
Oh ! if he'd only known the strength
   Of that warm love I cherish'd still !

I've walk'd for hours to and fro
   The gravel path —while drifting leaves
Fell round my footsteps sad and slow
   With rustling voice as one who grieves.

And then the winter came, with all
   Its dreary round of music, cards,
The well-remember'd county ball,
   And gossip measured out by yards.

And then the spring—each season seem'd
   To drag its weary steps along—
By no one ray of hope redeem'd,
   For Hope was dead, if Love was strong.

The spring was worst of all to bear :
    'Twas when the bursting buds were green
My heart had once most laugh'd at care,
    And thought life always seventeen.

The chestnuts blossom'd in their pride—
    White blossoms with a ruby streak—
And greeted summer like a bride
    With blushes on her fair pale cheek.

But I was wretched and alone—
    Starving because of love's great dearth.
O God ! if I had only known
    In those old days all love was worth !

Oh ! the heart-sickness of that time,
    The weary longing—hope deferr'd
Through summer sun and winter rime—
    For just one sweet forgiving word.

    *   *   *   *   *

Ah ! for the days when an angel's touch
    Turns all the dross of this world to gold,
When the heart with rapture thrills far too much
    For mortal bosom in peace to hold.

When a crystal beaker, fill'd with wine,
    Is held before th' enchanted sight,
And the meanest object seems divine
    Seen through its shimmering, rosy light.

The sunbeams creep round the window-sill,
    And flood with glory the walls and floor,
Jewell'd with colour their pure rays thrill,
    Forth from that beaker of wine they pour.

The shadows fall softly, subdued and sweet;
    Their darkest is only the tint that glows
The sky when the night and the evening meet,
    Or the deep, rich heart of the damask rose !

For the wine in that crystal beaker burns
    And sparkles, till joy has the radiance caught,
And lightens the shadows, till sorrow turns
    To the soften'd calm of a serious thought.

The essence of all that can make life fair,
    Or earth of heaven can realize,
Rich, strong, potent, is there, is there
    Held by mortal hand, seen by mortal eyes.

But drain the beaker!   Its wine was meant
  To gladden the very heart of man,
One glorious bumper of deep content!
  Then find the charm of life ye who can!

The gods' own nectar was that one taste,
  And Paradise was in its draught empearl'd ;
'Tis over! and now what a dreary waste
  Seems this hard, workaday, cruel world!

What is there left ?   Is the magic spell
  Gone with the draught of that wondrous wine?
Ay, all is over! we know full well
  The beaker we hold is no longer divine.

Only a frail, empty glass, through which
  The world is seen in its poorest light,
Nothing to soften, to brighten, enrich ;
  Only the chill and the shadows of night!

Quench'd are the sunbeams in drizzling rain,
  The gold proves nothing but base alloy,
For life is shadow'd by doubt and pain,
  And sorrow is sorrow—though joy's not joy.

SUNLIGHT.

A few drops linger—the last poor drain
   Of all that made life and existence dear ;
They only linger to leave a stain—
   Love's memory is but a sting and tear.

Ay, dash the beaker to atoms now !
   Another draught it will never hold ;
And dream not idly, with aching brow,
   But face the life that is yet untold.

Dreary and desolate waste it may seem,
   But 'tis the same as it was before,
There is but missing the wine's red gleam,
   'Tis but our hearts that are wrung and sore.

We have but paid, as we all must pay !
   For, 'till the earth is itself removed,
Earth's sons and daughters will every day
   . Learn how soon *love* passes into " *loved.*"

      *   *   *   *   *

Two years pass'd over : much the same
   Was every day and every year ;
But no new love nor passing flame
   Had made the memory less dear.

When this year sank into decay,
  My dear old " grannie " went to rest :
She pass'd as peacefully away
  As leaves dropp'd on the brown earth's breast.

No lingering illness—but a calm
  And quiet sinking into sleep :
Her day's work done—an evening psalm ;
  And I was left alone to weep.

Life's strands are changes such as these :
  Before the chill New Year began,
My Uncle Guy was at The Lees,
  And I was living with Aunt Anne.

Her house was harsh and strange to me,
  Train'd up in such a different school ;
Once silken bands of liberty—
  Now icy form, and iron rule.

A third spring came with heavy tread ;
  This spring I was to spend in town :
Will lost—and dear grandmother dead,
  I too, like him, regret will drown.

PART II.

GASLIGHT.

<center>~~~~~~~~</center>

LONDON.

THE London season was just at its height !
  Talent, rank, beauty, and fashion had met ;
Old age, defying Time's venomous spite ;
  Youth with the dew on her roses still wet ;
Hearts wearing out with life's struggle and fret ;
  Lips laughing lightly at sorrow and care—
Folly, sin, passion, mirth, love, etiquette,
  Jostling each other in Vanity Fair.

'Twas Aunt Anne's carnival : all through her life
  She loved the world, and the world had loved her—
Treated her kindly as maiden and wife,
  Married her daughters without a demur ;

Slander itself could not utter a slur—
　　Always immaculate, always correct ;
No scandal clung to *her* skirts like a bur,
　　Fraying the edges with mute disrespect.

Take her as she stood before me each day,
　　A well-preserved widow of sixty or less ;
Clear, well-cut features ; hair silvery grey ;
　　Sweet plaintive smile that could volumes express ;
Hands whose light touch was itself a caress ;
　　Voice low and cooing as pigeon's love-tales ;
Faultless in manners, appearance, and dress,
　　But hard as stone which the downy moss veils.

Wisest of chaperons surely was she
　　(Keener wits never man's fortress attacked)—
Sifting out every floating *on dit,*
　　Till information was sound and compact.
How she finessed ! with what infinite tact
　　She'd ascertain every tittle and jot—
Carefully separate fiction from fact,
　　Then pronounce who was a "match" and who not.

Lord Henry's good, but Sir Perkin in debt ;
  Young Chobbs acknowledged a real millionaire—
Plebeian blood is a drawback, and yet
  Self-made men push their way now everywhere.
Lord Baynham's charming, but people declare
  That—well – he isn't a marrying man ;
Nor is Lord Standish ; though Ida St. Clair
  Means to secure him—if any one can.

Ere long two " matches " like moths flutter'd up,
  Singeing their wings at Aunt Anne's beacon-light,
Sipping with rapture the Circe-charm'd cup,
  Graciously proffer'd them every night.
One—old Lord Meguelin—stately, upright,
  Rich as a Crœsus, and only threescore
(Courtship is such a fresh innocent sight
  When the bride chosen will rank No. Four !).

Second, Lord Dalesford, of whom it was said,
  He had ten fancies for every hair
Torn off by Time from his very bald head,
  And, with those counted, five hundred to spare ;

Past forty now, he eluded each snare
  Spread by the wily to capture his heart,
And was wont often to coolly declare
  He cared for nothing—save flowers and art.

No girl could suit his fastidious taste,
  So matrons said (their girls doubtless had tried);
He was not one who would marry in haste
  Any fair wife his kind friends might provide.
Then came a laugh and a whisper aside—
  Aunt Anne smiled sweetly, unmoved and serene;
But sweetest tempers, if ruffled, can chide,
  And *I* was treated to many a scene.

" You are so careless in playing your cards ;
  The way that you waltz'd with Frank Barton last
    night,
Knowing he is but a ' sub ' in the Guards,
  Is worse, dear, than silly—such things are *not right ;*
Any one bless'd with good sense and good sight
  Must know Lord Dalesford is thinking of you ;
Yet though he says you are lovely in white,
  Every evening you wear maize or blue."

Sometimes my sins were too much for Aunt Anne ;
　She'd pass the day on a sofa reclined,
With a scent-bottle, a novel, a fan,
　Weeping real tears her lace kerchief behind.
Vainly I tried to be soothing and kind ;
　To all excuses one answer she gave,
" Ah ! May, I trust this won't weigh on your mind
　When you have driven me into my grave."

Then I would kneel down and give her a kiss,
　While she in low wailing accents would say,
" How can you dare to be wicked like this,
　Knowing Lord Dalesford's the match of the day ?
When I was young no girl *dared* disobey
　Those who were able to guide and direct :
Now all the teaching is tending one way,
　Signs of the times we are led to expect.

" Wish you to marry a man you don't love !
　Don't use such dreadful expressions to me ;
Well-bred girls love those their guardians approve,
　Making affection and interest agree.

Oh ! that I've lived such an hour to see,
    Setting yourself heaven's goodness to baulk ;
Really, 'tis almost like flat blasphemy :
    There, leave me, May, I am too ill to talk."

Thus it went on until, weary, heart-sick,
    I found it wisest to calmly agree ;
Tired of waiting, and stung to the quick
    By Will's persistent avoidance of me,
I resolved I would forget him, and, free,
    Follow Aunt Anne's never-erring advice—
Marry Lord Dalesford, and thus let him see
    Others were proud of me—at any price.

So, to my lover's delighted surprise,
    All at once I took a different cue,
Blushing a little, and dropping my eyes—
    "One more waltz ?"—*yes*, then—" I can't refuse *you*."
What if I felt it was hollow, untrue,
    With my love still in my heart's core impearl'd,
I brush'd off the thought as noon brushes the dew
    From fast opening buds ;—'tis the way of the
        world.

When I felt I was nothing to him,
   In the deep sense which makes true love divine !—
Only a hobby, a fancy, a whim,
   Like his old china and pictures and wine ;
Something whose sparkling glitter and shine
   Caught his artistic, fastidious eye :
What did it matter ? the substance was mine ;
   I could afford to let shadows go by.

What if I knew he was nothing to me !
   He whom I soon gave the tenderest claim ;
He'd to good settlements doubtless agree,
   And I should share his position and name.
Who is there would not have acted the same ?
   Hearts do not break now-a-days—they're too tough.
These were sufficient excuses to frame,
   There—*I had done it*, and that was enough

    *   *   *   *   *

One more success my revered aunt could boast !
   Soon our engagement was duly " arranged,"
Duly announced in the next *Morning Post*,
   Will and I now were for ever estranged.

Yet, in my heart were old memories ranged,
    Like Indian idols on some holy shrine,
Worthless as wood—till devotion has changed
    Every puppet to symbols divine.

Not that I murmur'd—I'd chosen my fate,
    With my own hands mix'd the draught I must drink;
Snatch'd at the grandeur, the pomp, and the state,
    Daring all—save to be quiet, and think ;
Knowing that though from the step I might shrink,
    Drawing back now was quite out of my power ;
Better, by far, snap the past's broken link,
    And court excitement to drug every hour.

The day came at last when, friends crowding around,
    A bishop presiding and blessing the sale,
Love's knell in the clang of the joy bells was drown'd,
    And flowers were strewn on the past's haunting trail.
If holiest vows were but lip-made and frail,
    My diamonds lent them a brilliant disguise,
And falsehood, wrapp'd up in a Brussels point veil,
    Is decently clad—in society's eyes.

Married!   'Twas over.   The future lay hid
  In life's fresh volume of fair bridal white.
Ah! for how many, on raising the lid,
  Angels the language of paradise write!
Not so for us.   Some mist, filmy and light,
  Floated between us in word and in thought.
Slight was the barrier—cobwebs are slight—
  But in its meshes was happiness caught.

I did not deem love in the contract at all ;
  Enough if I gratified Lord Dalesford's eye :
To him were as verjuice, and wormwood, and gall,
  A badly match'd colour—a ribbon awry ;
Fastidious and carping, each error he'd spy—
  My coldness seem'd nought to an ill-fitting glove ;
The *bric-à-brac* trifles his money could buy,
  A matter far greater than friendship or love.

His soul was so fill'd up with Wedgwoods and coins,
  With pictures and cameos, artists and art ;
The tie which two natures in one union joins
  But drifted us farther and farther apart.

Some promising *protégé* he meant to start
   With all gracious patronage duly in life,
Became, for the moment, the slave of his heart:
   What room could he spare for the claims of a wife?

Neglected I was not—unsatisfied? yes.
   The thrill in the voice and the glance of the eye,
The fond, foolish phrase and the silent caress—
   Mere trifles for which women hunger and die—
These were not for me. Thus a year glided by—
   A year that ambition had reign'd in love's stead—
And still from my heart came that clamorous cry,
   "Stones—stones everywhere—I am starving for
      bread!"

Oh! woman, the curse that your mother call'd down
   Is surely summ'd up and completed in this:
To sicken with dread at a man's surly frown,
   To tremble with joy at a man's clinging kiss;
To lose sight of self is your glory and bliss;
   As pearls are in vinegar melted, ye would
Dissolve your whole life and existence in *his,*
   Though not worth one drop of your loving heart's
      blood.

Yet yours the revenge ! in each spoilt, ruin'd life,
   'Tis rarely a woman has no share or part ;
And ground in the hands of each frail, faithless wife
   Is always the something which man calls a heart.
A venom-barb'd arrow—a poison-tipp'd dart—
   Is wielded by many a shallow coquette ;
Both bitter and keen is the lingering smart—
   Too slight to complain of, too deep to forget.

     *   *   *   *   *

One day Sydney came in great triumph to me
   About a young artist he praised to the skies,
Whose style, touch, and colour were something to see,
   Whose talent must strike the most ignorant eyes.
This time he was sure he'd discover'd a prize—
   No arrant impostor like Franklin or Grey ;
He gloried in helping true genius to rise ;
   And so on, so on—in his usual way.

'Twas nothing to me ; but I just heard him out—
   By courtesy civil, yet bored all the same ;
'Twould end as all *protégés* ended, no doubt,
   With neither the patron nor artist to blame.

Upon *me* such matters had so slight a claim,
   I took them as one takes inflictions *perforce*,
Nor troubled to ask the new prodigy's name.
   "Oh! coming to luncheon!" "Receive him?" "Of
      course."

How often a sentence which changes our fate
   Thus off the tongue glibly, unconsciously slips;
I walk'd to the window, observed he was late,
   And watch'd the slow raindrops' monotonous drips.
Ah! why did there run to my sheer finger-tips
   That strange, sudden shudder—that vague, name-
      less thrill?
"Good God!" the words sprang like a scream to my
      lips,
   My husband's young artist was—it must be—Will!

I glanced round in terror—Lord Dalesford had gone;
   So no one had heard my wild, passionate cry:
One minute—all trace of emotion had flown—
   I gave Will my hand without tremor or sigh;

Remarking by chance, when my husband was by,
  We *had* met before, but 'twas some time ago.
"Four years." "Is it really? How fast time does
    fly!"
"You've altered a little." "I'm older, you know."

Alas! 'tis a lesson most learn—while a storm
  Shakes every mainspring of life to its source,
Calmly to go through each orthodox form ;
  Smiling and chatting as matters of course :
The last Paris fashions, the "favourite" horse—
  Eyes, lip, voice, manner, by long practice train'd ;—
No one would dream with what terrible force
  Every heart-chord to breaking is strain'd.

From then we met often—Aunt Anne was away—
  And no one in town knew our broken romance ;—
Lord Dalesford was more and more charm'd every
    day ;
  More and more was I thrown with him—*are* such
    things chance ?

He painted my portrait, and strove to enhance
  Each natural charm with the true painter's skill ;
Once more lit my eyes with the old roguish glance—
  The glance that belong'd to youth, spring-time,
      and Will.

Vainly we tried for a time to disguise
  Facts too apparent to heart and to sense ;
Vainly we tried to be guarded and wise ;
  Vainly we courted each shallow pretence :
For, as if seen through a powerful lens,
  Trifles the greater significance gain'd ;
Then came a moment—sharp, crushing, intense—
  Telling us all our nonchalance was feign'd.

How I remember that day ! for its sting
  Lashes like Furies' fierce scorpion cords.
We were alone—no unusual thing ;
  Sydney had gone with his sister to " Lord's,"
When Will said suddenly, sharply (the words
  Cut through the silence like some keen-edged knife
Ripping asunder life's holiest chords) :
  " May ! you're not happy as Lord Dalesford's wife."

Then all my long pent-up sorrow burst forth,
  As the ice melts at a touch of the sun,
When his rays glow in the far frozen North,
  Telling that summer and warmth have begun—
All the distress I had hinted to none
  Flow'd in a torrent of passionate speech—
Unreserved speech—to the one, only one
  Whose lightest words to my soul's depths could
    reach.

Then, as he drew my head down on his breast,
  And my eyes droop'd 'neath his passionate kiss,
One weary moment my heart seem'd to rest,
  Quietly yielding herself up to bliss.
Had I not hunger'd and thirsted for this?
  What weigh'd with this were position and name?
This—that through life I seem'd fated to miss,
  Or grasp to find it but sorrow and shame.

Wives who have married the " man of your heart!"
  Girls pure as snowdrops just kiss'd by the frost!
Turn not away with a shuddering start,
  Thinking me utterly hopeless and lost.

Not yours the life by your own folly cross'd ;
  Not yours the passion-wrung anguish of soul :
Only the shipwreck'd, by wild tempests toss'd,
  Know with what fury the mad billows roll.

'Twas but a moment my head rested there ;
  Then, with an effort, I shook myself free,
Bidding Will go, with the strength of despair,
  Since he could never be lover to me.
Meekly accepting Fate's iron decree,
  I bade him farewell—heart-broken and sad,
Never once doubting that he would agree,
  When he said sharply, " Why, May, are you mad ?

" Loving me thus with your whole heart and soul,
  Knowing that I would dare all for your sake,
Can you thus calmly your feelings control ?
  No, May ; *this* time there is too much at stake.
Surely you've courage your bondage to break,
  Or your love 's paltry and flimsy indeed !
You own your marriage at best a mistake ;
  Then 'tis no marriage at all in my creed.

"Ah! that you love me, my darling, is plain ;
  Speak to me, May! tell me not to despair ;
Tell me you're mine, and mine only, again,
  Pledged mine for ever,—as one time you were.
I go to Italy—*come with me there ;*—
  Dalesford will instantly seek a divorce :
Once safe, my treasured one—safe in my care—
  No one shall part us by intrigue or force."

Slowly, but surely, the sense of his words
  Flash'd their full meaning on heart and on brain :
With the mute strength which conviction affords
  When danger stands out both certain and plain,
"Go, Will!" I cried, half distracted with pain ;
  "Though I *do* love you, I've sworn to be true ;—
Leave me, in mercy—you tempt me in vain :
  I *cannot* do it !—not even for you !"

"And yet you love me!" he said with a sneer,
  Flinging me from him with almost a curse ;
"This is the love you hold ten times as dear
  As your lord's title and bravely stock'd purse !

So you are his, are you—better and worse?
　　Hold to him, then, and lull conscience asleep;
Thinking the form 'twas a lie to rehearse
　　Makes it a marriage 'tis sacred to keep.

" Yes, think it *marriage*,—the whole time you turn
　　Shuddering away from your husband's caress;
Think it is marriage, whenever you yearn
　　For me—not him ; poor fool ! he will not guess;
Say it is marriage—nor dare to confess
　　That you have sold yourself.   All things are right,
If church, and priest, and society bless,
　　Making it marriage in God's and man's sight.

" Think yourself blameless, though to *me* is given
　　All the love shrined in your heart's very core;
Think yourself holy, and pure, and forgiven,
　　Though you are acting a lie—nothing more.
Fling me aside—you have done it before,
　　And you have made me whatever I am ;
Leave me to swear, as in those days I swore,
　　Truth is a fable—religion a sham !

"That *is* religion! Stand fast to it, May;
  Leave me to fight out life's battle alone.
What does it matter to you? You will say
  (Plaintively sighing, in sweet, saint-like tone),
'Ah! 'tis the devil's own tares he has sown;
  And as he sows—so, alas! he must reap.'
Yet the hand giving the tares is your own—
  Satan is choice such an agent to keep."

Silently I bore each harsh, biting word;
  Silently I look'd a farewell to him!
Though my heart throbb'd like a wild, frighten'd bird,
  Though the fast-falling tears made my eyes dim—
Though my brain seem'd in confusion to swim;
  Still I was resolute—until he said,
"May, you are shaking in every limb;
  Is it the parting with me that you dread?"

"Will!" I wail'd out, in my passionate pain,
  Stretching my hands out in utter despair,
"Don't leave me thus—though you tempt me in vain;
  Your scorn and hatred are too much to bear."

"Yet," he said, " not for my sake will you dare—"
    He paused—and his face wore a dark, angry look :
We both heard my husband's light step on the stair,
    And heard him call cheerily, " Are you there,
        Brooke ? "

How that night pass'd and the next morning came,
    Or how the morning became afternoon,
I hardly know.   To my over-wrought frame
    Sleep refused even the chariest boon.
But as I watch'd the soft midsummer moon
    Fade in the darkness which heralds the day,
And darkness yield to the sunlight of June,
    I pray'd that thus might my night pass away.

Two weeks glided by.   To my husband's surprise,
    We saw and heard nothing of Will all the time ;
I thought he had left me—and thus, in my eyes,
    Mere crafty neglect became honour sublime.
I knew not then all the foul refuse and slime
    Which Love gathers when as a reptile he crawls ;
I thought Love wing'd straight from the heavenly clime,
    Forgetting an angel is lost, if he falls.

One evening (Lord Dalesford had gone out alone—
    But I pleaded headache, too weary and ill
To talk, laugh, and jest in my usual tone,
    Like convict compell'd to a social tread-mill ;—
The house was unusually quiet and still—
    My thoughts far away in my old childish home)—
The door open'd softly : I felt it was Will.
    "Well, darling," he whisper'd, "you see I have come!

" I leave town to-night ! there is no time to lose.
    Come with me, my sweetest—nay, don't turn so
        white ;
I give you this once, and but this once, to choose :
    You keep or forsake me, as you will, to-night.
I've all things in readiness, so that your flight
    May not lack one comfort devotion can give.
Look up, my heart's treasure, and tell me I'm right—
    That you are mine—*mine* for as long as you live !

Then, as my lips tried to frame a reply,
    Once more around me his strong arms were thrown.
" Can't you relinquish me, Blossom ?   Don't try—
    Breaking my heart, you must first break your own.

                        X

Think "—and his voice took a soft pleading tone—
    " Think of the long dreary vista of life
If we must spend it apart and alone :
    Come with me, May—in my eyes you're my wife."

But as the drowning, in one swift review,
    Live their past lives in a moment of time ;
So flash'd upon me in that moment, too,
    Memories unsullied by sorrow or crime ;
Like perfumes wafted from some favour'd clime,
    Like music breathing of heaven and peace,
Like Sabbath bells, in a sweet evening chime,
    Bidding the conflict of passions to cease.

It seem'd as though, once more an innocent child,
    My mother's clear voice taught me God's holy law,
Beneath trouble's lash to be patient and mild,
    And copy one life without blemish or flaw.
And then, as in some dreamy vision, I saw
    That mother borne down by long anguish and pain,
Her pale lips still breathing, as I gazed in awe,
    " Don't grieve for me, *Blossom*, we'll soon meet
       again."

Meet again! ah! my mother, the dust of the
    world
  Had smother'd the jewel you taught me to
    prize;
I carried Christ's banner in silence, and furl'd
  That banner you bade me display to all eyes:
But, though for long ages a diamond lies
  Dust-cover'd and lost, 'tis a diamond still;
So faith, once implanted and nurtured, will rise
  Superior to passion or mere human will.

My mother! if ever pure spirits are sent
  To watch o'er the loved ones they held dearest
    here;
Then surely your spirit that hour was content
  To leave for a moment its happier sphere.
The step stood out boldly—unvarnish'd and clear;
  No more Satan shone as an angel of light;
I sprang from the arms that were only too dear:
  "Leave me, Wilton," I said; "I will not go to-
    night."

His lips turn'd first white, and then sheer ashen
    grey !
  "You mean that ?" he said. ."Ay, God help me,
    I do."
" Then may every curse light on you from this day,
    Whatever you suffer is only your due."
Without one last look — without one last adieu —
    He left me ; and I — I remember no more :
The bright gaslight paled to a dim, sickly hue ;
    And then — I sank in a dead faint on the floor.

PART III.

FIRELIGHT.

HAZELMERE.

DOES trial kill?   I hardly know.
　　Some weary ones perchance may die,
Struck down by many a bitter blow ;
　　But I know none such—nay, not I.

I lived, and lived on much the same
　　(In outward seeming) as before
Will, like a tempting serpent, came
　　With fair fruit poison'd at the core.

But still I think I tried to be
　　A truer woman, better wife ;
To win my husband more to me,
　　And join more fully in his life.

And time brought blessings in his train ;
  For, like a flash of heaven's own joy,
With April showers of freshening rain,
  God sent me my own precious boy.

For one long night I lay with life
  Just trembling in death's awful scale ;
While strength and pain waged fearful strife,
  And art and skill they fear'd must fail.

I lay there without count of time,
  And met death boldly—face to face ;
Till, robb'd of dread, it seem'd sublime
  To win all through my Saviour's grace.

I had no strength to argue out
  Theology or doctrines wild ;
I simply lay without a doubt,
  And trusted as a little child.

Was that my husband at my side ?
  My husband, with those anxious eyes ?
Was it *his* voice in anguish cried,
  " May God take me too, if she dies " ?

I could not think about it much,
  My head was weak ; but still I knew
An angel's hand with hallow'd touch
  Had rain'd me manna down as dew.

They held some cordial to my lips,
  And Sydney holding me, I drank
With effort a few faltering sips ;
  And after that—there came a blank.

The morning was breaking grey and chill,
  The rising sun streak'd all with red,
When I awoke, to find that still
  My husband knelt beside my bed.

His arm still held me ; he'd not stirr'd
  A muscle, lest that quiet sleep
Should be disturb'd by sound or word :
  Thus only love a watch can keep.

The doctor's fingers on my wrist,
  As they had rested, rested yet ;
While surely Sydney fondly kiss'd
  My lips, with " Don't speak yet, my pet."

But all was dreaminess to me—
    A sort of restful, peaceful maze ;
I lay there quite contentedly,
    Half dozing, many, many days.

My baby, nestled to my breast,
    All fresh from heaven, had won me this
Sweet, soothing sense of perfect rest,
    And tinged each weary hour with bliss.

Then, as my strength I slowly gain'd,
    And as the soft spring days grew long,
One haunting memory remain'd,
    Like words of some forgotten song

Which, ghost-like, float through heart and brain,
    Yet never gather form nor tune—
Vague as a foxglove's low refrain
    When fairies dance beneath the moon ;—

For as the summer onward wore,
    And peaches caught the sun's bright gleam,
My husband grew reserved once more,
    And proved it only was a dream.

    *   *   *   *   *

I was not much in town that year,
　My health was frail—the season short ;
So down at leafy Hazelmere,
　Or Laurel Lodge, we two held court.

We two—I mean my boy and I ;
　My boy ! the fairest eyes could see,
Who, as the summer weeks flew by,
　Grew dearer every day to me.

A rosebud opening to heaven,
　Stealing from angel's lips its hue,
Untouch'd by this world's soiling leaven,
　But gemm'd by morning's earliest dew ;

A snow-flake ere it falls to earth,
　Pure gold unmingled with alloy ;
So from the moment of his birth,
　So fresh, pure, precious, seem'd my boy.

　*　　*　　*　　*　　*

The autumn leaves began to turn
　To russet gold and red-vein'd brown ;
Crisp grew the heather and the fern,
　And hedges donn'd their scarlet crown.

The teeming orchards paid their store ;
　　The harvest yielded up its grain ;
And in the cover, on the moor,
　　The sportsmen's guns were heard again.

We were alone—some guests had left,
　　And others were as yet not due ;
So I to my loved nursery crept
　　To steal my boy an hour or two.

The early twilight darkening fell,
　　As off my bonny prize I bore
To quarters that he loved right well—
　　The rug upon the library floor.

I see it now ! that dear old room—
　　Its crimson curtains, big oak chair,
The deep recesses fill'd with gloom,
　　And dim, dark portraits here and there ;

The wide old-fashion'd hearth ; the dogs,
　　Whose sturdy brazen arms have held
For many centuries Yuletide logs,
　　And every phase of life beheld.

I stirr'd the fire up warm and bright,
    Till far its flickering flashes glow'd ;
And, revelling in its warmth and light,
    My baby laugh'd, and kick'd, and crow'd.

" Ah ! boy," I said, while many a shower
    Of kisses on his lips I laid,
" Who gave these tiny fingers power
    To heal the wounds the past had made ?

" Who, when I hunger'd so for love
    I almost snatch'd at sin and shame,
Because they tried my heart to move,
    Because they seem'd to bear love's name—

" Who sent you, darling, pure and sweet,
    To love me, little one, and make
Life's path less weary for my feet—
    Existence happy, for your sake ?—

" God sent you, precious ! Do you think,
    You, who are fresh from angel's lore,
That you will ever be a link
    To make your father love me more ?

" You have his eyes, my baby boy—
　　The same deep eyes of earnest grey ;
But yours meet mine with kindling joy,
　　While his are coldly turned away.

" Do you think, in the days to come,
　　Your wee, weak hands will ever bring
The spell which turns house into home,
　　And make my heart with gladness sing ?

" Not even *your* love stills, as yet,
　　That aching, hungering, yearning cry
For ' something more.'   Ah ! well, my pet,
　　You'll be more, won't you, by-and-by ? "

The answer came—but not from him :
　　In the recess behind my chair
The shadows gather'd dark and grim,
　　Had hidden Sydney lounging there.

'Twas his voice said, " My wife ! my wife !
　　I'll love you—have loved—*loved* you, sweet !
Why, you are more to me than life,
　　My very soul is at your feet.

"And you can speak like this!   Oh, May!
    How can I find the words to touch
Your heart aright—find words to say
    That I have loved you—ay, too much?

"*Too much!*   My very love for you
    Has made me careless.   Wife! oh, May!
Thank God I sat and listen'd to
    The words that I have heard to-day."

Speechless I listen'd!   Could this be
    My loveless husband—careless, cold—
These burning words!—could this be he
    So self-absorb'd, reserved of old?

"You *cannot* love me!"—this at last
    Burst from my lips—"you could not be
So callous through these three years past
    If you had ever cared for me."

"Callous! my wife! by heaven, no!
    'Twas you who, cold as ice, repell'd
Each word or look which strove to show
    The warmth and love my bosom held.

" I could not rave as many do ;
    I could not flatter ; could not swear,
With all my earnest love for you,
    None were so faultless or so fair.

" You women like a man who raves ;
    But some men, May, can barely speak ;
For deepest feeling utterance braves,
    And words are strong where love is weak.

" *I* could not even speak my love—
    It lay too deep, my wife, for speech ;
But hidden fires volcanoes move,
    And trifles subtlest problems teach.

" Could you not see, with woman's tact,
    How my whole nature yearn'd and pined,
In every thought, and word, and act,
    Some sympathy of yours to find ?

" Failing, I sought with double zest
    The old pursuits, to deaden pain—
To leave, heart-sick, the hopeless quest,
    And court forgetfulness in vain.

" But judge if I have loved you, May ! "
  Then, crossing to his secretaire,
Among some papers laid away,
  He took one letter out with care.

" Read this," he said.   The firelight glare
  Flash'd on the handwriting—the date ;
And coals of fire they truly were,
  To scorch and brand with livid hate.

Kneeling upon the hearth, beside
  My baby innocent, I read
How Will in baffled rage had tried
  To wreak his vengeance on my head.

" I leave for Rome," the letter ran,
  " Because I love your wife too well ;
I have no fear of any man,
  And will not stoop a lie to tell.

" You ask the reason—there it is !
  I am no whining, craven cur,
Who dare not own a thing like this ;
  And if you doubt me—*question her.*"

Much more—much more there was—I read,
　　Till sickening terror o'er me crept,
Till heart and brain were dull as lead,
　　And life seem'd in a chasm cleft.

But as I read, upon the past
　　The light of truth began to dawn,
The spell of long years faded fast,
　　And love was changed to loathing scorn.

This, then, was my heart's own elect!
　　And this the idol past all price!
So prized that peace and self-respect
　　Were incense for a sacrifice!

This was the wondrous love which burn'd
　　To have the first—the only claim;
First offering ruin—and, that spurn'd,
　　Striving to blacken and defame.

This truly was true love's own self!
　　A china lamp with soul within;
Lord Dalesford's was but coarsest delf—
　　Mere common love, not even sin.

Again I read the letter through
    Before I utter'd a defence :
Oh ! could my husband deem this true ?
    Would he believe my innocence ?

Wine-red I flush'd with burning shame,
    Deep scarlet to my very brow ;
For home, and husband, and fair fame
    Seemed trembling in the balance now.

I think it would have weigh'd me down.
    And crush'd me into dumb despair :
But, plucking at my velvet gown,
    Two baby hands came like a prayer :

And as the goaded tigress turns,
    And dares e'en fire to save her young—
So, when a mother's fond heart yearns,
    Words spring unbidden to the tongue.

" Sydney," I said, " as God can hear
    Each, every word I utter now,
This child is not more pure and clear
    Than I, of broken marriage-vow.

"Long years ago—(he does not say
  That we were lovers years ago)—
I loved him well; and yesterday
  I even might have told you so.

"I loved him well—too well, may be,
  But never wickedly.   'Tis true
He dared to speak of love to me ;
  I listen'd—and was leal to you.

"Your coldness drove me to despair ;
  I listen'd—ay, for half an hour :
Can you look in my face and swear
  You never felt temptation's power.

" Unloving, weary, and unloved,
  I loathed my splendid, gilded life ;
But no temptation could have moved
  My sworn allegiance as your wife."

" I see !" he said—not bitterly,
  But as we say harsh things when true—
" You stay'd from principle, and I
  Would give my life for love of you.

" You thought me callous, cold, unkind ;
   Ah, May! if you had loved *me* more,
You scarcely could have been so blind,
   Or laid such charges at my door.

" You wrong me there ! I loved you so—
   What pleased you, pleased me : when that lad
Brought back your bright cheeks' mantling glow,
   And mellow laughter, I was glad.

" You did not seek him—it was I
   Who threw him daily in your way ;
Foolhardily, unconsciously,
   But not from want of love, my May.

" You did not love me—that I knew—
   While you were more to me than life ;
But yet I never doubted you :
   How *could* I doubt my honour'd wife ?

" And then there came that awful blow !
   But even then, so true was I,
No shock could lay my heart's love low,
   No jar could shake my loyalty."

Slowly I raised my downcast eyes,
   And bless'd the fire's uncertain light :
He mark'd the hot, quick blushes rise,
   And read th' unspoken words aright.

" I answer'd that, my wife," he said,
   " As best 'twas answer'd.   But for you—
How could I call down on your head
   The blame that chiefly was my due ?

" I forced the truth from out that hound
   (I could have murder'd him that day,
And should, I think, had I not found
   That you were innocent, my May).

" *Let that go by.*   Two years or more
   Have pass'd since then—no need to tear
Old sorrows open to the core,
   When new-born hope is brooding there.

" I do not ask you for your love—
   Not now—but only for my due :
All that has happen'd—does it prove
   His love or mine was most for you ?

" Who do you think has loved you best—
    That villain, with his selfish snare,
Or he who holds you to his breast,
    And deems his wife's best haven there ? "

Trembling I raised my burning face,
    And such a loving glance met mine,
That, folded in his close embrace,
    'Twas like a draught of cordial wine.

I nestled in those sheltering arms
    So close—yet closer, closer yet ;
For every touch sent heaven's own balms
    To heal the past's long standing debt.

A calm stole softly o'er my heart,
    A peace crept gently in my life—
Till grief and I were far apart,
    And rest seem'd in that one word—wife.

That such a noble heart should beat,
    And beat for me could scarce be true ;
Yet life seem'd finish'd and complete—
    Complete, and yet begun anew.

I tried to speak, but on my tongue
  The trembling words half-sobbing died ;
And closer, *closer yet*, I clung,
  In answer to my husband's side.

Thus, only thus, could I express
  How my whole soul was moved and stirr'd ;
How my heart thrill'd at each caress,
  And throbb'd at every loving word.

And ere my boy's impatient cry
  Recall'd me to this lower world,
The future, with a smile and sigh,
  The past's dark wings for ever furl'd.

    *   *   *   *   *

My eyes were open—every day
  Taught me to prize my husband's worth,
To see the gem which hidden lay
  Beneath the trifling things of earth ;

Taught me to break away the crust
  Of shy reserve and nervous pride ;
Taught me to yield most perfect trust—
  And trust and love are near allied ;

Taught me to bear with every whim,
  Till whims and fancies ceased to tease ;
Taught me to be so proud of him,
  My only thought was—how to please.

It was not love, but gratitude !
  It is not summer when we see
The primrose hiding in the wood,
  To court the shy anemone ;

But when the spring flowers kiss, we know
  The birds will soon begin to sing,
And fervent summer's noontide glow
  Will follow in the wake of spring.

What *is* love ? Yielding all ; for thus
  We lay our hearts upon a shrine,
Whose very dust can be to us
  As something sacred and divine.

And gratitude ? Life's chalice filled
  To overflowing. At a touch
The generous wine is freely spill'd,
  Because we cannot give too much.

When sunset on the bleak hill-side
His parting benison has given,
We gaze, and hardly can divide
The blush of earth from glow of heaven.

So, lit by fire from above,
Till self dies slowly in the flame,
Pure gratitude will melt in love,
Changed wondrously—and yet the same.

From out the wreck of shatter'd years
Our guardian angels oft arise ;
My girlhood's disappointed tears
Had built this rainbow in the skies.

Dark thunder-clouds oft usher in
Those warm sun-rays which glow and shine,
And sparkle, till the cold drops win
The changing hues of hope's glad sign.

.   .   .   .   .

Those days were very calm and sweet.
Alas ! earth's brightness does not last ;
When joy flings roses at our feet,
The step of sorrow follows fast.

I dare not even now recall
  That fearful time of anguish'd pain ;
For hot, quick tears would blinding fall,
  And grief rise fresh and strong again.

Grief does not die—she only sleeps,
  To waken at a sound or touch ;
Too often ceaseless vigil keeps,
  Lest we should slight her power too much.

The sunlight dying in the west,
  The wafted breath of new-mown hay,
A well-known air, an idle jest—
  And past years are as yesterday.

On me she lays her fingers light,
  And at my heart begins to knock,
If in the silence of the night
  I hear the loud old nursery clock.

I could not bear to have it moved—
  Its stands there, and shall stand my time :
Its noisy tick my baby loved ;
  He crow'd with laughter at its chime.

But once, as it struck half-past three,
    One, two, full strokes, subdued and slow,
Such misery was dealt to me
    As laid my very spirit low.

My boy lay still, and I knelt by—
    For human skill her all had done;
And I re-echoed David's cry—
    "O Absalom! my son! my son!"

His laughing eyes were glazed and fix'd,
    His struggling breath kept awful time
To that old clock, which slowly tick'd
    The moments to the half-hour chime.

No other sound the silence broke
    That labour'd breathing—harsh and long—
And that old clock, whose every stroke
    Seem'd doubly loud, and doubly strong.

Then came a heaving, gasping sigh;
    And then the clock tick'd on alone—
Save for my wild, heart-rending cry;
    For I was left—and he had gone.

And then it seem'd as though the sun
  Would never shine for me again ;
As though fresh life had but begun
  To herald in the fiercer pain.

It seem'd as though I was bereft
  Of all and everything ; my life
A curse, which fate in twain had cleft,
  To keep the peace, and leave the strife.

Could I have lived throughout that trial ?
  I think not, but my husband's love—
Unfailing as the widow's phial,
  Unchanging as the stars above—

Crept round my heart : it wrapp'd me up—
  Sustaining, cheering, comforting ;
It forced the bitter from the cup,
  It drew the poison from the sting.

By its own force it made me turn,
  As needles to the loadstone yield ;
By its own strength it made me yearn
  By love to have love's absence heal'd ;—

Till, with the gather'd strength of years—
   No childish fancy, girlish dream—
But swell'd by woman's deepest tears
   Into one broad, resistless stream,

My love flow'd out to meet his own ;
   And joining in a boundless sea,
One from the other was not known—
   I all to him—he all to me.

     *   *   *   *   *

One evening as the firelight's glare
   Upon the library portraits play'd,
A step came ere I was aware—
   A hand was on my shoulder laid.

Two lips were press'd up close to mine—
   As often, often now, they're press'd—
When loving fingers closely twine,
   And heart secure in heart can rest.

The silence was too sweet to break :
   'Tis when we live the nearest heaven.
Our lips are mute ; the sounds they make
   For this world's use alone were given.

We yearn until we almost catch
    The rustling of the angel's wings
Which bear the boon we strive to snatch
    As foretaste of the heavenly things.

We yearn—for panting heart and brain
    A glimpse of paradise would see ;
But one word brings back earth again,
    And all earth's dull reality.

Perchance in worlds more blest than this
    The icy chains of speech may melt—
Our lips may learn the words they miss,
    And speak what here is only *felt.*

'Twas Sydney who was first to speak :
    " I've something, love, that you must see."
His voice was faltering and weak,
    And his arm clung *so* close to me.

" What is it, darling ? " and my head
    Droop'd nestling on that well-loved breast.
" 'Twas in this morning's *Times*," he said ;
    And closer yet my hand he press'd.

" I have it here."   The firelight glare
     Flash'd on the *Times,* as once before
It flash'd on words which seem'd to tear
     My heart-strings open to the core.

My eyes caught one familiar word,
     Then eager glanced along the line :
" At Florence, on the twenty-third,
     John Wilton Brooke, aged twenty-nine."

*   *   *   *   *

I leant back slowly in my chair—
     Those few brief words a spell had wrought,
And, like mute shadowy forms of air,
     The past years as by magic brought.

I saw the old familiar room ;
     I saw the dancers in their glee ;
I saw the chestnut's pearly bloom ;
     I heard Will's whisper'd words to me.

I saw him satisfied, content ;
     I heard his wild, ambitious schemes,
How life should in great deeds be spent
     With me—the idol of his dreams.

I saw him as he was that day,
  A lad of promise and of parts,
Whose self-will'd, fearless, dashing way
  Went straight to all the women's hearts.

I saw his reckless, boundless pride,
  Which scoff'd at, knew not self-control ;
Which would with Lucifer have vied,
  To forfeit heaven or gain the whole.

I saw each uncurb'd fault stride on
  With giant steps, till, in a trice,
The glamour screening them had gone,
  And every fault became a vice.

Yet through all beam'd that strange, sweet smile
  Which never failed a friend to win—
Which won you, though you knew the while
  It cloak'd but selfishness and sin.

Through all there came that nameless charm
  Which few could question or repel ;
The influence which, for good or harm,
  Had seldom fail'd to serve him well.

Ah, Will! your splendid gifts might claim
  A man's best powers to employ;
Yet, in your hands, your life became
  A spoilt child's broken, ruin'd toy.

*   *   *   *   *

I think we all forgive the dead,
  However great may be our wrong;
Like sweetest perfumes, on them shed
  The charity withheld so long.

Death's scythe a slip of ground divides,
  And peace flies upwards as a dove;
Earth, like a tender mother, hides
  Her children's faults with pitying love.

And blame me not, if then there fell
  Upon my hand two lingering tears;
They came as water from a well
  Forgotten—ay, moss-grown for years.

They came—a tribute to the past,
  A memory of its purest, best;
For death a sheltering veil had cast
  With reverent hand o'er all the rest.

FIRELIGHT.

The trembling Magdalene was saved,
 The thief felt mercy's boundless power,
And he who pardon humbly craved,
 Found rest at the eleventh hour.

"God give *him* rest !" I whisper'd low ;
 And as I met my husband's kiss,
I felt what had *I* done to know
 Such perfect happiness as this ?

"God grant *he* made the better choice !"
 And sweeter far than words or pen
Can half express, my husband's voice
 Responded tenderly, "Amen !"